COUNTDOWN TO ARMAGEDDON!

"Primary launch sequence initialized," the loudspeaker announced. Spidey saw Captain America push forward even harder through the surging mass of villains on the floor below, clearing a pathway with fists and feet—but the control panel was still out of the Avenger's reach. "Ten second standby. Nine. Eight. Seven . . ."

Just let me get to the keys, Spidey thought. Let me get there.

Spider-Man reached the key on the left-hand side of the panel. He pulled away the unconscious body of the man who had turned the key in its lock, and reached out to twist it back. The lock snapped back to Unarmed—but the synthesized voice wasn't counting any longer. It was saying something new.

"Missile armed. Engage primary launch system. Missile away."

GLOBAL WAR

Martin Delrio

Illustrations by Steven Geiger and John Nyberg

BYRON PREISS MULTIMEDIA COMPANY, INC.

NEW YORK

POCKET BOOKS

NEW YORK · LONDON · TORONTO · SYDNEY · TOKYO · SINGAPORE

An *Original* Publication of POCKET BOOKS

 POCKET BOOKS, a division of Simon & Schuster Inc.
1230 Avenue of the Americas, New York, NY 10020

Copyright © 1996 Marvel Characters, Inc.
A Byron Preiss Multimedia Company, Inc. Book

Byron Preiss Multimedia Company, Inc.
24 West 25th Street
New York, New York 10010

The Byron Preiss Multimedia Worldwide Wed Site Address is:
http://www.byronpreiss.com

ISBN 0-671-00799-8

First Pocket Books paperback printing January 1997

10 9 8 7 6 5 4 3 2 1

Edited by Howard Zimmerman
Cover art by Mike Zeck and Phil Zimelman
Cover design by Claude Goodwin
Interior design by MM Design 2000, Inc.

Printed in the U.S.A.

GLOBAL WAR

Nightime in New York City.

A red-and-blue blur swung swiftly through the concrete canyons. Spider-Man was on routine patrol, enjoying the evening's quiet, until—

The urgent blaring of car horns from below him broke through his reverie. A sudden squeal of brakes was followed this time by the heavy thud of two cars trying to occupy the same space at the same time.

Spidey shot a web-line down to a nearby billboard and swung around a corner. There he spied the strobing blue lights of a police car, heading in his direction at top speed. A siren pierced the air, its rising and falling tones warning everyone to stand aside, the law was coming through. But the police car wasn't headed for the site of the wreck that Spidey had just heard. It was following another car, a long, low sedan.

"Whoa, Nelly," Spider-Man said, shooting another web-line up and behind him to halt his forward progress.

The sedan was painted a dark blue-black that glistened dimly beneath the streetlights. It took the next corner at speed, its rear skidding around in a four-wheel drift as the driver refused to slow his frantic pace.

"Going somewhere in a hurry?" Spider-Man said, and turned to swing rapidly after the speeding vehicle. "Up here I don't have to worry about the stop lights."

In the street below, the police car took the same corner, siren warbling and lights blazing at their maximum. The tires squealed, and a stink of burning rubber drifted upward.

From his vantage point near the rooftops, where he easily kept pace with the dark car, Spidey observed the chase. The police weren't falling behind, but they weren't gaining, either. From farther uptown another siren blared, as reinforcements summoned by radio hurried to the scene.

Then Spider-Man saw something that he hadn't expected. The police car beneath him wasn't the only vehicle involved in the chase. An Army deuce-and-a-half—a two and a half ton truck, painted in camouflage colors—was bringing up the rear, its gears growling and its exhaust pipe spewing diesel smoke. The canvas cover arched over its rear end flapped and billowed with the speed of its passage.

"Quite a party," Spider-Man mused. "First New York's Finest show up, and then a bunch of Uncle Sam's own. J. Jonah Jameson doesn't know it yet, but I think he really wants a picture of whatever this is all about."

While his right hand was busy with a web-line, Spidey used his left to click his belt camera over to auto-shoot. High-speed film might get some decent shots even in this low light. He'd find out in the darkroom in the morning.

The object of all this pursuit, the dark sedan, continued on its course westward across midtown. The web-slinger matched its course and speed from five stories above. The speed of the chase had increased. Rather than just swinging freely, Spider-Man had to put some muscle into the task in order to keep up.

The road ahead of the sedan lay clear for a moment. Then from the right and from the left more sirens blared. One block ahead, two police cars came from uptown and skidded to a halt, nose to tail, blocking the intersection. There they sat, an imposing barrier, the blue lights flashing from their roofs and dancing off the upper windows of the buildings that towered on every side.

The sedan didn't even slow down. Instead, the driver aimed for the rear quarter of the first police car. He struck it squarely, the center of the sedan's front grille smashing the cop car's fender just above the left rear tire.

Sparks flashed in the darkness, and the dull boom of the impact muted for an instant the high keening of the sirens. Glass shattered—a brittle, high-pitched note—and the headlights of the sedan went out, smashed by the collision. But the driver shoved down on the gas at the moment of impact and the dark sedan kept on going as the police car spun away.

Then the fleeing car was through the roadblock and still rolling. The pursuing police car didn't slow down, but followed the sedan through the gap it had cleared. Then the Army truck arrived on the scene. Wider than any of the other vehicles involved in the pursuit, it hit the already-damaged police car a glancing blow as it sped through the narrow gap without slowing down.

Then the fleeing car was through the roadblock and still rolling.

Whoever that is, Spidey thought, is serious about getting away. And the good guys are real serious about stopping them.

The Hudson River was approaching as the little parade sped west. More sirens sounded from every direction as the police answered the call for backup.

Smoke was coming from the damaged tire on the getaway car, mingling with steam from the radiator. The car was wobbling as it sped through the Manhattan streets, and the police were gaining. Ahead, along the river, Riverside Drive was a mass of flashing lights.

Then, with a sharp report like a rifle shot, the dark sedan's damaged tire gave way, exploding in a complete blowout. Fragments of rubber flew everywhere. The nose of the sedan dipped to the right, and sparks shot upward as the wheel rim gouged into the blacktop. Then the sedan spun sharply to the right, cutting across the Drive, and turned over.

It rolled three times before coming to rest on its crumpled roof. Spider-Man quickly turned and swung down to the ground. Having run out of buildings from which to swing, he was now faced with the daunting task of dodging cars that sped along the Drive in order to reach the wreck.

Gas poured from the ruptured fuel tank on the vehicle's bottom, now turned up to the sky like the belly of a dead beetle. Streetlights cast harsh shadows beneath the wrecked car. The leaking gasoline spattered on hot metal and erupted in a gusher of flame that enveloped the whole wreck.

Incredibly, someone was moving amid the shattered glass and crumpled steel. Like some crazed Olympic gymnast, Spidey vaulted onto the highway. Without pausing, he leapt, flipped, jumped and tumbled his way past speeding vehicles.

But before Spider-Man could get to the crash scene, three men crawled out from openings which had once been the car's windows. They were dressed all in black, with masks covering their faces. Two of them carried cases of some sort. They scattered in different directions. Spider-Man had taken a step toward one, getting ready to cast a web over him to prevent his getaway, when his attention was drawn back to the car. Someone was still caught inside the flaming mass.

Spider-Man leapt forward, ignoring the flames even as their intense heat penetrated the cloth of his costume. The driver of the sedan was still caught, pinned behind the steering wheel. He struggled, but was unable to free himself from the debris.

"Hold on!" Spidey shouted. "I'll get you out!"

Using his incredible spider-strength, the web-slinger reached down, grasped the edge of the driver's-side door and ripped it off. A pool of burning liquid crept closer to his legs as he pushed the car back, rolling it half onto its side to get at the trapped occupant, crumpling the roof still farther as he did so. With his free hand Spidey reached in and grabbed the driver and pulled him out.

Then he felt his spider-sense tingling!

Spidey threw himself backward, clutching the rescued driver to him as he rolled away. Behind them, the car exploded in a lurid fireball, engulfing the entire passenger compartment in searing flame.

Spider-Man laid the person he had just rescued on the pavement away from the pool of burning gasoline. Then, at last, he looked up, no longer intent on his rescue mission. The police had arrived. The burning wreck was surrounded by police cars, and uniformed officers were converging on the scene. More sirens sounded in the distance, growing nearer. Fire trucks and ambulances, Spider-Man supposed.

"No time to lose," he said. He pulled the mask off of the weakly moving person on the ground. The mask, he realized, wasn't just a disguise. It was some kind of gas mask, or a rebreathing apparatus like a SCUBA diver would wear.

In the flickering light, Spidey was able to see, somewhat to his surprise, that the getaway driver was a woman. The gas mask had concealed her long blonde hair.

"What's this all about?" Spider-Man asked his prisoner. "Who are you?"

The woman didn't reply.

"Who sent you? Who are you working for?"

Spider-Man only had a few moments to find out what he needed to know before the police arrived. Being a costumed crime-fighter didn't get him any special relationship with the New York City police.

"Oh—oh . . ." the woman said, her eyes half opening. It wasn't a groan, Spider-Man thought. It sounded like she was trying to tell him something.

Then the woman's head lolled back as she lapsed into unconsciousness. Spider-Man stood, and turned to the approaching officers. Behind the police he saw a squad of Army soldiers, wearing helmets and flack jackets, fully combat armed, leaping over the sides of the deuce-and-a-half. The soldiers trotted toward him, their M16s at high port, ready to sweep up to firing position.

"Say, there," Spidey called out in his cheeriest voice. "Did you bring the marshmallows?"

"Stand clear of the prisoner," said a young man wearing camouflage patterned fatigues. Lieutenant's bars in subdued black graced his shirt collar. A .45-caliber automatic pistol was in a holster on his hip, but the flap of the holster was unsnapped and the lieutenant's hand was on the pistol's grip.

"Can you tell me what's going on?" Spider-Man asked.

"That's classified," the lieutenant snapped. "You don't have a clearance or a need to know." He turned to a man standing beside him. "Sergeant, secure the prisoner. And keep that . . . that *civilian* away from him."

"Her," Spidey corrected.

The sergeant stepped forward. "Doesn't matter. Still our prisoner."

"I'm ordering you to leave before I have you arrested for interfering in a federal matter," the lieutenant barked at Spider-Man. He looked tight-lipped, and not at all like somebody whose day had been made complete by the assistance of a friendly costumed wall-crawler. "Leave. Now."

"Nope, no marshmallows," Spider-Man said to himself, as he shot a web-line high to a corner of the building facing him, and swung up into the night.

CHAPTER
—2—

Near Broadway, Spider-Man paused to rest on the cornice of a skyscraper. Something about the driver's black uniform was tickling at the back of his memory. That black head-to-toe garb, topped with a mask . . . Spidey shook his head.

"I'm getting old," he muttered. "Memory's the second thing to go. Before you know it, I'll be talking to myself."

He cast a web-line to the south, and swung off. He was heading for the campus of Empire State University—ESU—where he'd first spotted the chase in progress. Maybe he'd find some clues there as to what this was all about.

The sky was going a lighter purple in the east by the time he arrived. Sure enough, the normally sedate urban campus was in an up-roar. Armed soldiers stood in front of all of the buildings, while an entire squad of soldiers ringed the science building, where Peter Parker—Spidey's alter-ego when he was being a normal student rather than a costumed crime-fighter—attended classes. Men and women dressed in conservative dark suits—which weren't uniforms, but which identified them as government personnel just the same—were interviewing students who had been on the streets when the incident took place.

All of the entrances to the campus were now guarded, either by city police or uniformed soldiers, or both. But gate guards presented no problem to a web-slinging Spider-Man.

Spidey looped a web-line from the library, swung across the student union, and came to rest head down, clinging to the wall of the science building about two stories up. He'd been no more than a swiftly darting shadow against the darkness.

Two of the suits were standing and talking quietly on the steps below him, down near the building's main door, making it seem like a great place to find out what was at the bottom of the disturbance. Spidey inched down the wall head first, getting what would have been a dizzying view for anyone without spider-powers.

A good thing no one ever looks up, Spidey thought as he crawled nearer and nearer. The two suits were just below him, but he hadn't made a sound. Now he could hear bits of their conversation.

". . . suppose they were after?" one of the men asked his companion.

"It's a mess down there," the other replied. "It'll take a while to figure out what's missing."

Down there? Spider-Man asked himself, puzzled. In the science building?

Whatever had happened looked like it had started in the sub-sub-basement, and Spidey already knew what was on the bottom level of the science building. Everybody on campus did. The government lab funded by the Department of Agriculture for research on turning cow manure into gasoline additives was a standing joke at the university. Word among the work-study students who had to carry crates of cow manure around in return for tuition credit was that it was the most boring place on campus, not to mention the most malodorous.

"They were in and out in a heartbeat," the first agent below Spider-Man was saying.

"We had troops on the ground in five minutes, and they were already leaving."

"They must have known what they were looking for," the second said. "Do you think they were after Clementine?"

"I hope they weren't. If they have it, we're in a world of . . ."

They broke off. A man was approaching. Spider-Man recognized him as the young lieutenant from the crash scene. His squad followed behind him.

Spider-Man felt the tingling of his spider-sense, that uncanny knowledge that some kind of danger was heading in his direction. Carefully, quietly, he began to inch his way back up the wall.

"Did you get them? What did you find out?" the first agent asked the approaching officer.

"Apprehended one," the lieutenant said. "Three others escaped, but the police are combing the area. They'll find them soon."

"They'd better," the second agent said. "This isn't an ordinary case. What was in those files could be the key to a real disaster."

From cow manure? Spidey asked himself. Something here was starting to smell bad, and it wasn't the crates of bovine by-product that students at ESU had been carrying back and forth for the past several years.

The lieutenant's gaze traveled up the wall. He focused on Spider-Man.

"He was at the wreck!" the lieutenant shouted, pointing at the wall-crawler. "Now he's here. He's one of them!"

The lieutenant's right hand scrabbled at his holster while his left pointed at the rapidly retreating form of Spider-Man. "Capture that wall-crawler!"

"Sorry, I've got a previous engagement," Spidey said, shooting a web-line upward and getting ready to swing.

"Halt or we fire!"

"Gee, that sounds almost unfriendly." Spidey pushed off from the wall, swinging back into the growing dawn. The young officer had raised his hand and was aiming his pistol at Spider-Man. Spidey shook his head. "Ah ah ah, can't have that. Wasting government property, to wit, a bullet."

With that, he shot a glob of web-fluid down at the startled officer. The sticky mass filled the gap between the pistol's hammer and firing pin as the man squeezed the trigger. Rather than a bang, the weapon made a soggy plop as the hammer got hopelessly jammed in the webbing.

"Don't feel bad," Spidey called back, as he looped another web-line and swung out wide of the troops. "People have been trying to shoot at me for years. None of those other guys had a lot of luck, either."

By now the squad had their weapons up, as the officer shouted, "Fire! Fire! Stop him!"

A ragged volley rang out. The troops were well trained—their fire came in bursts of three to five shots—but by now Spider-Man was web-slinging away, and making a difficult target.

"Anyone would think they didn't like me," he muttered as the bulk of the Recreational Arts building came between him and the rifles. "I'll be back to find out what's at the bottom of this, though."

He swung out in the direction of his downtown apartment, where his photographer's darkroom was waiting for him, along with the everyday clothing he wore as Peter Parker, science student at ESU.

Meanwhile, not far from the Hudson River docks, a group of three men came together. They were dressed in black jumpsuits and high boots; their faces were covered by tight-fitting masks.

"Think we lost them?" the tallest of the lot

whispered to his companions. His name was
Scudder, and he would have had a criminal
record longer than most people's resumes—if
he hadn't been good enough at his work that
most law enforcement agencies had never
heard of him at all.

The shorter of the two men Scudder had
addressed looked up and down the alley they
were in. A dumpster blocked the narrow brick
walls of the alley at one end. At the other
end the alley dead-ended in a soot-blackened
concrete slab. A rusty iron ladder on the
right-hand side of the alley led up to the roof
of the building.

"I think we lost them as soon as we sepa-
rated," the shorter man said. "The trackers
worked okay, getting us together. Has anyone
seen Leadfoot?"

Scudder shook his head. "I don't think she
made it out of the car."

"Bad luck for her. The boss isn't going to
like it. Hope he doesn't take it out on us."

"As long as we got what we came for,"
Scudder told him, "the boss won't mind
about anything else."

"Talking about something else—who was
that guy in the red-and-blue long johns?"

"The red and blue—" Scudder laughed. "I

By now the squad had their weapons up, as the officer shouted, "Fire! Fire! Stop him!"

forgot, Rusty. You're from out of town. That's Spider-Man."

"Is he a problem?"

"Only if he gets in the way. Now let's get to headquarters. The boss will want to have the stuff." Scudder hefted the briefcase he was holding. "We went through too much to get this. Let's move."

The three men turned to the ladder and began to climb. Halfway up to the roof Scudder leaned aside to push a discolored brick. A section of the wall swung back to form a dark opening. One by one the three black-clad men stepped off the ladder into the doorway. When the last of them had gone through, the door swung shut again. From the alley it once again looked like the grimy wall of an old brick building, identical to thousands of others in New York.

Inside the passageway, lights blazed up the moment the outside door closed with a snap of hydraulic locks. Light flooded down from recessed tubes in the ceiling. It showed walls of gleaming white synthetic material, and a floor of resilient foam plastic that deadened the sound of their footsteps. A thin haze of grayish smoke curled around their feet, the only outward evidence that the passageway was filling with an anti-intruder knockout gas.

The men in their breathing masks were un-affected. Silently the three walked forward, around a corner. A light flashed and a speaker beeped as each passed an identity-scan plate. Then they came to an open circular room, its only obvious exit the archway through which they had entered.

"I hate this part," Rusty complained.

"Shut up," said Scudder. "You know what to do."

"Yeah." Rusty took a clear plastic con-tainer from a recessed holding locker opposite the point where they had entered. He opened the container and the other two men put their briefcases into it. Then he closed the lid and turned the thumbscrews on each of the con-tainer's edges until he couldn't twist them any farther. "Right. Ready."

The lights in the chamber went out, re-placed by perfect darkness. At the same mo-ment the floor beneath the three men slid away, and they went falling, tumbling, down into the black.

Their fall was broken with a loud splash as they fell into water. Their momentum kept them going down. They slowed, then stopped, only inches above the bottom of the area they had fallen into. There, they paused. This place wasn't totally black. Tiny dots of light, like sickly lightning bugs, were buried on the bottom. The three men swam along, following the dots of light.

The bottom sloped down; the men continued swimming along the trail of light. If they hadn't known what to look for, the markers would have gone unnoticed. Had any of the swimmers been carrying a light, its glow would have drowned out the faint glimmerings. As it was, the men passed through an underwater labyrinth, as corridors and passages opened right and left, above and below them. It was a defense constructed to baffle ordinary divers, should they get this far, leaving them lost in the maze with their air running out.

Now the men came to a pressure door with a locked wheel in the center. Scudder placed his right hand into an indentation by the side of the wheel. With a loud snap the lock clicked over and the wheel spun by itself. Rusty and the third man pulled the door open and they all swam in.

The door closed behind them as the chamber they had entered filled with red light. The water drained away with a blast of cold compressed air. Mist blew through the chamber.

Rusty clutched the watertight box containing the briefcases.

When the water level dropped beneath his shoulders, Scudder pulled off his mask. He was handsome, in a craggy way, though his eyes were cruel.

"A good thing you didn't lose that on the way over, Rusty," he said, pointing to the container. "The boss wouldn't have a sense of humor about it."

"The boss doesn't care that one of us gets killed," said the third man, who had just removed his mask, "but he *does* care about those stupid papers!"

"Shut up, Deason!" the tall man hissed, whirling to face the speaker. He sloshed knee-deep water as he turned. "The boss can hear you. And he does *not* have a sense of humor. I can guarantee that."

"We're all tense," Rusty said. He too had removed his mask, revealing the red hair that gave him his nickname. "It was a long night, and we're all shook up that Emmy didn't make it. It could have been any one of us. But we're here now. So let's just go on in, finish the job, and see what the boss has got for us next."

Scudder and Deason had been eyeing each other warily. Now the tall man let out his breath and said, "Yeah. Let's get this over with."

All the water had drained from the chamber. They walked through an inner door into what was clearly a large underwater base. At a bank of lockers they stripped off their damp black jumpsuits and pulled on quilted jackets against the chill in the air. Other men and women, similarly dressed, came and went through crossing passageways. A low murmur of some public address system broadcast orders in a female voice.

"Do you suppose any of the sleepy-gas is still in there?" Rusty said, hooking his thumb at the box.

"Not enough to hurt us," the tall man said. "Come on—open it up. The boss is waiting."

The catches came open. Rusty took the top briefcase while Deason took the other. Scudder led the way along a passage where closed watertight doors opened at odd intervals. They paused before one, as unmarked as the next. The door opened automatically. They stepped in and the door closed behind them.

The room was empty except for a long wooden table and a set of viewscreens, large and small, ringing the room and covering the ceiling.

"You have them?"

The voice came from everywhere and no-where at once. The viewscreens began to swirl in shades of blue and green that reminded Scudder of the colors of a week-old bruise.

"Yes sir," he replied, keeping his eyes down, away from the unsettling screens. "What you sent us for."

"Lay the papers on the table. Face up. I must see them."

Rusty and Deason helped Scudder open up the briefcases and pull out sheafs of paper. They arranged the papers on the long slab of wood, side by side, covering it like some kind of typescript tablecloth.

The picture in the viewscreens swirled and coalesced into the shape of a man's shoulders and head. He wore thick glasses that nearly covered his pudgy round face. His skin had the pallor of a man who seldom ventured into the sun, and his dark hair lay straight, hacked into an ugly bowl cut and plastered against his skull.

"Yes," the man said, leaning forward to see better through the viewscreens. A hundred images, large and small, leaned forward looking at the table from all angles.

"Yes!" the voice exulted. "You have done well. What I needed is here."

A metal tentacle rose behind him, whipping

the air. It was joined by two others in front, as if they were eager to reach out through the viewscreens and seize the papers at once. "You have done well, gentlemen."

"Thank you, sir," Scudder said.

Rusty added, "Thank you, Doctor Octavius."

CHAPTER

—3—

Otto Octavius—known to the police and the press the world over as "Doctor Octopus," the sinister mastermind of a hundred criminal enterprises—had once been a quiet but brilliant research scientist specializing in nuclear chemistry. Then a lab accident had merged his robotic handling arms with his body and put them under his mental control. And all his brilliance had turned to twisted schemes of revenge and world domination—schemes that had, far too often, been thwarted by Spider-Man.

"Boss, there was a problem," Scudder said. His voice was low, as if he were unwilling to break in on Doctor Octavius's exultation.

"Was there any difficulty with the pickup?" Doctor Octavius asked.

"We wrecked the car."

"No matter. I have many," Doc Ock said. He turned back to studying the papers spread out on the table under the two-way view-screens.

"And Leadfoot got caught."

"A risk you were all aware of. Nor does it concern me—she knows nothing of any use to the authorities." Ock was growing impatient.

"She got caught by Spider-Man."

"Spider-Man! That odious arachnid has stuck his snout into my business one time too many. How did he know? What was he doing meddling with you? If someone talked . . ."

Doc Ock's face, which had been pale, grew redder and redder. Deep creases appeared in his pudgy cheeks. His teeth clenched and his lips drew back.

Scudder took an involuntary step back from the nearest viewscreen. He was a heartless thug, a paid thief and a killer for hire. But this much rage contained in a man as rich and powerful as Doctor Octavius meant that someone was going to be in deep trouble . . . and soon.

The four adamantium tentacles that sprouted from Ock's waist lashed in response to his fury. If he could have reached through the screen, Scudder thought, someone might have gotten hurt right then.

But, as abruptly as it had begun, the fit of rage ended. Only the tightness of his lips showed that Otto Octavius was still struggling against strong emotion. Now that he was coldly examining his options, though, he had become truly dangerous. Scudder was relieved that the storm was over, but concerned that perhaps—just perhaps—Doc Ock might blame him for being spotted by Spider-Man.

"It does not matter," Doc Ock said. His voice was level, lacking all inflection. "This is an opportunity. I shall take this gift that fate has offered to me, and use it to destroy Spider-Man once and for all. He cannot escape this time, for I will guide him to his destruction."

Octavius looked out of the viewscreen at the three who had brought the papers. "Leave me now, to study what you have brought me," he said. "Return to your quarters and await further orders—and those orders will come soon! *Then* I will deal with Spider-Man."

At that very moment, the object of Doctor Octavius's interest—dressed not in a colorful

costume, but in jeans and a windbreaker—
was approaching the campus of Empire State
University. Dawn had come with the sun rising over the Atlantic Ocean, the clouds turning a delicate pink and then white as the
golden orb rose in the east. Peter Parker was
on his way to class.

Along the way he intended to try and find
out what had happened on campus the night
before. A high-speed car chase through the
streets followed by gunfire in the middle of
the night couldn't possibly have gone unnoticed. In fact, it would probably be the talk
of the campus this morning.

Peter turned the corner beside the ivy-cov-
ered pillars marking the main gate of the campus. A police officer stopped him.

"Excuse me, sir," she said. "Do you have
ESU identification?"

"Oh, yes," Peter said, and pulled out his
student ID card with what he hoped was a
winning smile. The officer looked like she'd
been on duty at the main gate for a long time,
with a long time still to go.

"What's in your backpack?" the officer
asked.

"Just my books and some clothes," Peter
said, opening the bag. Sure enough, he had a
copy of Petersen's *High Altitude Particles*

lying on the top of a bundle of clothes. With his wife, Mary Jane, visiting her aunt in Florida, Peter was temporarily living the life of a bachelor—that meant doing his own laundry whenever he had a free moment. After his classes were through for the day, Peter's next intended stop was a laundromat.

"Okay," the police officer said. "You can come through, but please go directly to class, and when your classes are over, please go directly home. The campus is under security lock down."

"Thanks, sure," Peter said. "Can you tell me what's happening?"

"I don't know myself," the officer said, then turned to the young woman who had come up behind Peter and apparently wanted to enter the campus as well: "Excuse me, ma'am, do you have ESU ID?"

Peter walked through the gate. No one would suspect a costumed crime-fighter of entering so openly. It probably wouldn't even occur to most of the military and law enforcement types now crowding the campus that a super hero might have a valid university ID. But Peter didn't actually have a class to go to, not for a while. That would give him a little time to poke around, as long as he didn't look too much like a sightseer. He'd have to walk briskly from place to place instead of ambling and staring about, so that to a casual observer he'd look like a man who had a destination in mind and wasn't paying much attention to whatever else might lie along the way.

Peter had already noticed that there were a lot of police still around, and a lot of soldiers as well. Whatever had happened the night before clearly hadn't been resolved yet. Now he noticed something new. A barrier of yellow crime-scene tape was looped all the way around the science building. That had to mark the center of last night's action.

But what kind of action? Spider-Man wondered. Not even the theft of radioactive material would have brought this kind of response. Especially not the small amounts of low level isotopes held in the ESU science building. Peter was studying nuclear physics in that same building, and he was well aware of what was—and more importantly, what wasn't—present in the university's nuclear program.

Then, out of the corner of his eye, Peter spotted a flash of bright color: A tall, commanding figure dressed in red, white, and blue, with a glittering shield slung on his left arm. The man was still a good distance off, striding easily along, the pair of senior officers beside him almost trotting in order to match his pace. Peter recognized him at once. He was the most patriotic of all the Avengers, and one of the oldest super heroes still active in the city—Captain America.

That made sense. If national security was involved, and the President of the United States had called on the Avengers for help, Cap would be the one to respond. And Peter knew that J. Jonah Jameson would want photos of Captain America for the *Daily Bugle*. JJJ loved Captain America almost as much as he hated Spider-Man, and a photo of Cap on the job would be worth something.

Peter quickly unsnapped the miniature camera from his belt. He swung it up to his eye, focused, and shot two quick frames. He was snapping the camera back into his belt when he spotted Professor Guzman up ahead.

The professor also worked in the science building, and he looked upset that he wasn't being allowed to get near his own experiments. Guzman wasn't one of Peter's teachers, and might not recognize him, but Peter was willing to take that chance. He was certain that Guzman had seen him around the science building often enough to know that he belonged.

"Hi, Professor," Peter said, walking up to

Guzman. "Pretty wild what happened last night, wasn't it?"

Inwardly, Peter winced. That was a clumsy way to start an investigation. But he had to start somewhere. Reporters went around asking people stupid questions all the time, and people answered them. Peter had spent enough time around reporters at the *Daily Bugle* to pick up some of the tricks of the trade, and to know that they usually worked.

"Yes," Professor Guzman said. "I wish the police would get done so I can get back to work. I have some continuing experiments which, if not monitored, will be ruined. Six months' work!"

"Did you hear the gunshots?" Peter asked, hoping to work the conversation back around to current events, rather than continuing to dwell on the Professor's private woes.

"No. I was asleep, until *they* called about . . ." Guzman studied Peter for a moment, then waved a hand in a dismissive gesture. "Never mind."

"Well, I sure heard them," Peter said, wondering what it was that Guzman didn't want to say. "They" had called him in the middle of the night. Did that mean Guzman's own office was involved?

Peter decided to try out the one scrap of

hard information that he'd gotten through his earlier eavesdropping. "I wonder if this has something to do with Clementine?" he said, as if talking to himself—but loud enough to make sure Guzman heard.

"Could you wait here a minute?" Guzman said. "I just saw someone I have to talk with." The professor hurried off, taking one quick glance back when he'd gone twenty yards, as if to make sure Peter hadn't moved.

Bingo, Peter thought. Clementine it is. But I still don't know if our Clemmie is a person, a place, or a thing.

The tingling feeling of Peter's spider-sense came again. He looked toward where the professor had gone, and saw him talking with the pair of senior officers who had been escorting Captain America. As they spoke, Guzman raised his arm and pointed back in the direction from which he had come.

It didn't take psychic powers for Peter to figure out what the subject of their conversation was—and he didn't need an invitation to leave, either. Spending a week getting questioned by the military could take a bite out of his plans.

Peter turned and walked away as quickly as he could without drawing attention to himself. Explaining where he'd come by the name

"Clementine" was something he couldn't answer without revealing his secret identity. Since he wasn't about to do that, the investigators would figure out pretty quickly that he was lying to them about something. And after *that*, they'd start jumping to all kinds of wrong conclusions.

Peter ambled around a corner, and put on some speed. Maybe he could get lost in the crowd of early-morning students, most of them dressed as he was in jeans and a shirt. He'd have to lie low for a while around campus, he realized, but what else were libraries for?

"Halt!"

The shouted order came from behind Peter, delivered with such an air of command that he almost obeyed. He looked behind him. It was Captain America, all right, running toward Peter with a long, loping stride.

Peter's spider-sense wasn't tingling. Captain America wasn't a threat. He was, in fact, the best friend that anyone fighting evil could have. But Cap was Spider-Man's friend, not Peter Parker's. Being caught right now by Captain America would put an end to Peter's secret identity as surely as would getting caught by the Army.

Coming to a quick decision, Peter began to run.

Normally no one, not even a perfectly developed man in superb shape like Cap, could catch Spider-Man in a footrace. But Peter didn't dare use his spider-powers, not out in the open, out of costume, and in front of witnesses. Holding himself back was hard—he had to mimic the exact speed that would be believable for a grad student in good but not necessarily perfect shape. And while he struggled to find it, Cap was gaining. Slowly, but gaining. Peter could hear the red-white-and-blue Avenger's footsteps slamming into the ground behind him as he ran. Peter tried hard to avoid the temptation of leaping up the side of a building.

A building.

Peter cursed himself for forgetting that he still had one advantage, even though he didn't dare to use his spider-powers: He was intimately familiar with the ESU campus layout, and Captain America wasn't.

Like any longtime student, Peter knew where all the shortcuts were, knew which doors were locked at this hour, and which ones were open. He knew which classrooms were likely to still be empty, and—most important—he knew which of the structures on campus had been built before the invention of air conditioning had turned most buildings into stone boxes with tiny windows that no one but a custodian could open.

Rounding a corner, Peter put on a burst of speed. There, up ahead, was exactly the help he was looking for. The ESU economics building was a landmark example of late nineteenth century university gothic architecture. It was complete with functional gargoyles adorning all the rain gutters and waterspouts, and at this hour the departmental offices should all be empty. Peter cut left, sprinted up the broad granite steps, and ran into the building.

Coming to a quick decision, Peter began to run.

CHAPTER
—4—

Captain America plunged into the economics building after the student he had been pursuing, and halted. The darkened corridor was empty, and the fleeing student was nowhere to be seen.

Then he heard something—the sound of a window opening in the room immediately to his right. Cap dodged sideways through the door in a move that showed his complete mastery of combat skills. One of the tall windows on the far side of the room stood open to the morning breeze. The ring-pull of the large window shade above it still swung wildly back and forth, betraying the means by which someone had exited the room hurriedly only a moment before.

Cap put his star-spangled shield in front of him and dashed to the window. The muscles beneath his chainmail jersey worked easily. A glance out the window showed that his quarry was nowhere in sight. The young man was a fast runner, and clever, using his knowledge of the local terrain to good advantage. Cap placed a hand on the window sill and made ready to follow the trail before it grew cold.

Then he heard a slight noise above him on the outside wall, and twisted his head to look up. And there he saw Spider-Man sitting on the wall, the soles of his feet planted flat against the vertical brick surface, looking as comfortable that way as anyone else would look sitting on the ground. Spidey had his arms wrapped around his knees, and his eyes—or at any rate the sardonic white lenses on his mask—were turned toward Captain America.

"Spider-Man," Cap said. His voice was unsurprised. "Did you happen to see a young man—brown hair, backpack—come running by here?"

Spidey gestured across the lawn toward a stand of trees. "He went thataway."

Cap followed the gesture, and nodded. "Looks like the boy knows how to run."

Spider-Man remained crouched on the wall. "Yes, I suppose he does. He made a clean getaway."

"Right," agreed Cap. Now was not the time, he decided, to mention the object—almost certainly a backpack—that he could see webbed into place not quite out of sight behind one of the rain-gutter gargoyles. "Too bad. I had some questions I wanted to ask him."

"You'll probably run into him again one of these days," Spidey said. "But as it happens, I have a few questions of my own. Last night I saw this whole thing start, and I think I have a right to be active at the end of it — but I seem to be *persona non grata* in this burg. One of those soldier-boys tried to make hash out of me last night with copper-jacketed rifle slugs. Think you can keep them from trying to do it to me again?"

"I heard about that," Captain America said grimly. "I'll have a little chat with them about fire discipline and the necessity of enemy recognition routines."

"Wonderful. Glad to be working with you," Spidey said.

"Wait a minute!" Cap said. "I'm not teaming up with anybody—I just want to *talk* with you. I'm here under Presidential orders, and you are not part of the investigating team."

"When people crash police barricades in my town," Spider-Man said, "I get interested. And when I get interested, I stay interested. A character flaw, I'm sure, but there it is."

"Okay, okay. Let's talk somewhere else," Captain America said, resigned. "You may be able to perch all day sideways on a brick wall, but craning my neck out of a window isn't quite my style. I'll see you down in front of the building."

And a few minutes later, Captain America, a member of the mighty Avengers, and Spider-Man, a sometime-associate of that super-powered team, met on the broad granite steps of the economics building. The two men began to walk across the campus, side by side, deep in conversation.

"This investigation is far above the city level," Captain America said. "I'm handling it. And while I appreciate your help, especially in apprehending the injured driver, there's nothing more you can do."

"Well then," Spidey said. "How about satisfying my curiosity? You know that I'll just keep poking around if I don't hear what's been going on."

Captain America pinched the bridge of his

nose and shook his head. "Believe me . . .
I know."

"Okay. I know there was a break-in at a
government research facility that's located
here on campus."

"That's not exactly secret," Captain
America said. "And it's being investigated by
the proper authorities. We don't need any
assistance."

"Then you won't mind if I tag along. I love
watching pros at work."

"You'd just get bored and you'd only be in
the way," said Cap. "At this stage, the investigation is mostly routine legwork."

This is getting me nowhere, Spider-Man
thought. I wonder if the same thing that got
such a rise out of Professor Guzman will get
Cap to tell me what's up?

Aloud, he said, "Would it help you guys
out if I went off looking for Clementine on
my own?"

Captain America stopped and turned
toward Spidey, grabbing his arm in a steel-
like grip. "As of right now," Cap said,
"you're officially part of this investigation.
Now . . . please don't do anything crazy."

"You know me, Cap," Spidey said. "Would
I do anything crazy?"

The star-spangled Avenger released the

web-slinger's arm and turned toward the science building, which was still surrounded by its ring of troops. "I know you, all right. That's why I said it."

Spider-Man decided to ignore that remark. Instead he asked, "Why does a Department of Agriculture project on making methane out of waste products rate this kind of protection?"

"I'll tell you what I can," Captain America said. "The Department of Agriculture project was just a cover story. Anyone who came around looking would be shown some vats of really foul-smelling stuff, and the front people would talk about it all day. Kept out nosy reporters and kept the college administration happy."

"A cover story." It made sense, Spider-Man thought. He felt chagrined that even he—with his photojournalist's skepticism and his crime-fighter's instincts—had been taken in by it. "Covering what?"

"A Department of Energy project on alternatives to nuclear power," Captain America said. The science building was getting close. The senior soldier on guard recognized Cap and saluted him as he approached. Cap returned the salute without breaking stride, as he continued talking with Spider-Man. "Alternatives to nuclear power gave the project a reason to work with small amounts of nuclear materials."

Spider-Man's thoughts raced ahead. "But that was also a false trail, wasn't it?" Spidey guessed. "The DoE project was just the cover underneath the cover."

Cap nodded. "That's right. The Department of Energy project was cover for a Department of Defense project. The people in charge didn't think that anyone would be able to follow the trail that far down."

The two heroes entered the science building as Cap spoke. To their right, a stairway led down from the entry foyer into the building's lower reaches. The fire door at the top of the stairway was wedged open, but tied off with yellow crime scene tape. Cap and Spidey stepped over the tape and entered the stairway.

The first thing Spidey noticed was a security camera mounted on brackets on the wall. Someone had burned it out, perhaps with a laser. The camera's case was melted, and its lens was cracked.

Spidey nodded toward the bit of destruction. "It sure looks to *me* like someone saw through the cover stories."

Captain America nodded, then said, "Whoever did this job knew that we'd have troops on the ground in minutes. And they didn't care. Which says to me that they knew what they were looking for, and exactly how long it would take to find it."

The stairway led down several floors below ground level, deep into the sub-sub-basement. At the very bottom of the stairway was a corridor marked with OFFICIAL BUSINESS ONLY and KEEP OUT signs. A soldier with a rifle stood guard. Cap and Spidey passed by the guard and went on into a lab at the far end of the corridor. White-coated crime scene technicians were dusting the area for fingerprints while photographers recorded their work.

"Through here," Cap said to Spidey.

Another doorway led the two super heroes into a network of more corridors and additional laboratories. At last, they came to a room holding nothing but a set of filing cabinets. All of the cabinet drawers hung open, and where their locks had been were now only gaping holes. The papers the cabinets had held were all charred and blackened. The contents of other drawers had apparently been pulled out and scattered about on the floor. The room was a mess, with cabinet doors open, file folders scattered and burned, and all the metal furniture either torn up or partially melted.

The smell of burnt residue was strong here, and the floors were littered with paper ash. More technicians were carefully picking up the larger pieces of burned paper and ash—many of them still contained traces of typed words.

"Any progress, sir?" Captain America asked the uniformed officer in charge of the work. The man was a full colonel, with eagles on his shoulder tabs.

"It's going slowly," the colonel replied. "We're checking every scrap against a list of what was here to begin with, and it's going to take a lot of time before we know if anything is missing."

"So what makes you think that anything is missing?" Spider-Man asked. The colonel didn't answer—he seemed to share the attitude of the day toward non-government crimefighters—but Captain America pointed to the locks on the nearest cabinet.

"You see how it was melted open?" Cap said. "When that happens the metal splashes, and it makes streaks where the drops hit other surfaces. You see here?"

Spider-Man looked where Cap was pointing. "Those two brown lines?"

"Yes. Look where they cross. See how that one sloping down from the right is on top of the one that slants up from the left? That tells me that the one on the left happened first, left its line, then the one on the right happened. So I know which of these two locks was blown first. The same goes for all the other locks in this room."

"And you think that the bad guys went to the cabinet they were looking for first," Spidey said. "And then blew all the rest of them just to make things harder when you and your buddies arrived to clean up the place."

"That's right," Cap said. He walked across the room and pointed to an otherwise unremarkable cabinet, third from the left in a bank of identical cabinets. "This is the one that went first. And the papers that were in here—well, if they got out we could all be in a lot of trouble."

"Because they're about Clementine."

"Right. How much do you know about that system?"

Spidey looked down into the open drawer. "Nothing but the name," he admitted.

"That's more than most people in the world know," Cap said.

"We're not dealing with somebody like *most people*, then."

"It looks that way. When it comes to secret projects that have the possibility of destroying civilization as we know it, I don't believe in coincidence and random chance."

"So what *is* Clementine?" Spidey asked. "After a build-up like that one, I'm almost afraid to find out."

"You ought to be," Captain America said. "It's a missile system. They call it 'Clementine' because once it's fired, it can't be called back."

"Like the girl in the song," Spidey whispered. Understanding hit him, and he felt cold. " 'You are lost and gone forever'—*everything* is lost and gone forever—"

Cap nodded grimly. "That's right. 'Dreadful sorry, Clementine.' "

5

"It began as a sort of last-ditch defense to be used when nothing else is left," Captain America explained. "It's got a subsystem that prevents anyone from tracing the missile, tracking it, or shooting it down once it launches. When we abandoned the antimissile defense system back in the eighties, the Clementine system should have been shut down too. But it wasn't. The research went on. And it went on right here. The documents in that file drawer contained the list of Clementine sites . . . and the *go-codes* that someone would need to fire them."

Spidey had begun to recover his emotional equilibrium. Now was not the time to wonder how such research had come to be done at a campus in the heart of the city, instead of at a secret government lab out in the middle of a desert somewhere.

Probably because everybody knew about the secret labs out in the desert, Spidey thought. "So now you think that someone has that missile site list and those launch codes?"

"It would be foolish for me to assume anything else. Now I've told you what I know. It's time for you to tell me what you know."

"Okay," Spidey said. He quickly gave a recap of the events of the last evening. "I got one of them out, but I had to let the others go in order to rescue her."

"I can't fault you for your instincts," Cap said. "I would have done the same thing. The fact that those men were carrying cases tells me that they'd grabbed papers from here."

"There's something about the way they were dressed that was familiar to me," Spider-Man said. "But I can't quite place it."

"The military is working on finding out who leaked the information from here," Captain America said. "When they find out who told where the codes were, we'll be better able to trace the person who ordered this raid."

"Where are the Clementine sites?" Spidey asked.

"One's in Kansas, the other one's in New

Mexico," Captain America said. "They've both been ordered to full security alert, in case our unknown friends decide to go after them."

"Okay," Spidey said. "Do you have any theories about who could be behind this?"

"There are only about half a dozen countries advanced enough to use this kind of material and this information," Cap said. "Right now, the one at the top of my list is Latveria."

"Doctor Doom's country."

"Right. If Doom has Clementine, he could rule a good-sized portion of the world pretty effectively. Something else about Doom: intelligence summaries say that he's been importing a lot of nuclear material lately, and that his missile program has been put into high gear."

"So Doom is your most likely suspect?"

"I wouldn't say that. Just that we're looking in a lot of directions, and right now Latveria is one of them that we're looking at closely."

Right, Spider-Man thought. So Doom is your most likely suspect.

The technicians were still working on the scraps of paper. Every time they found a group of words they typed them into their laptop computers, looking for matches in the copies of the documents they carried. Each time a document was identified, they informed the colonel, and he checked it off on his list.

"I'm sorry, Captain America," the colonel said. "We haven't identified anything from the critical folders yet."

"I don't think we will, either," Captain America said. "I'm going to call this a Class-One security breach."

"I'll inform the president," the colonel said.

Spider-Man and Captain America left the room full of blasted filing cabinets. "There are still a couple of things I'd like to know," Spidey said as they went back up the stairs to ground level. "First, who was that woman I rescued last night?"

"Fingerprints identify her as Emmy 'Leadfoot' Katz," Captain America replied. "The best getaway driver on the coast. She isn't cheap to hire, either."

"Does she know anything about who hired her?"

"No. Just a voice on the telephone. She was hired for one night only, if her story is true."

"The truth and criminals aren't found together too often," Spidey said. She was about to identify someone last night, he thought. Even if she did think better of it by the time she made it to the hospital. "I think we're looking for a super-villain. With Doc Doom in the picture, that's almost certain."

"Don't make up your mind too soon," Cap said.

"Since I'm now a part of the investigation," Spider-Man said, "I think I'll go investigate. See you around."

As they exited the science building, Spider-Man shot a web-line to the roof of the ESU library. Captain America watched silently as the web-slinger swung away from the campus.

Spidey's path took him, ultimately, back to his own apartment, where he had a full dark-room setup. Once there, he removed his Spider-Man garb and became ordinary Peter Parker, freelance news photographer.

Photos take time to develop, and rushing the process can make unusable smears out of the best shots. Peter worked as fast as he could. By the time he was done, he had three prints that looked pretty good. One was of the dark sedan crashing through the police roadblock, viewed from above. Another was of the woman driver without her mask. The third was of Captain America at ESU.

I told Cap that I'd be investigating this my own way, and my own way involves stirring things up, Peter thought. And the great metro-

politan newspaper is the best way I know of
to stir things up. As long as I don't mention
anything secret, Cap shouldn't mind. Much.

By the time Peter emerged from the dark-
room with dried prints, the sun was now well
up, and the morning rush hour was starting.

Dressed as Spider-Man once again, Peter
loaded his camera with a new roll of film.
Using his favorite exit—the bedroom window—he made his way downtown, swinging
easily from his web-lines. He'd deliver the pic-
tures to the *Bugle* on his way to campus. Sure,
it was the long way around, but that wasn't
a problem for someone whose favorite route
was high above the crowded streets.

At the *Daily Bugle* building, Spider-Man
ducked behind the oversized letters of the
Bugle rooftop sign and changed clothes.
Then, as Peter Parker, he walked down the
two flights of stairs to the newsroom. Editor
Robbie Robertson met Peter at the door to
the city room.

"Hi, Robbie," Peter said. "Get a story
about the police action on the West Side
this morning?"

"No, I don't have a story," the editor replied. "The guys on the police beat say that
their contacts all clammed up. 'Routine traffic
stop.' With fire trucks, wreckers, ambulances,

traffic snarled for hours, and more rumors than you can count. Routine traffic stop, my foot. But we don't print rumors. Unless I have two independent sources, JJJ will have my head. And my job."

"Think you could go with this?" Peter asked. He slid the photos out of their protective envelope.

Robbie looked from one print to the other. "These are great, Peter. How do you get this kind of thing, anyway?"

"My methods are my own," Peter said. "I know I'm not a reporter, but . . ." He hesitated.

"Don't hold back, Peter," Robbie said. "If you've got something to say, then say it."

Peter pointed to the photo of the female driver. "Well, one of my . . . sources told me that this woman is a professional getaway driver known by the street name 'Leadfoot.'"

"Interesting," Robbie said. He turned to the third photo. "What's this?"

"I took that one on the campus at Empire State University, this morning. That's where the chase started. Captain America's taking command of the investigation."

"You're golden," Robbie said. "We have something for the morning edition after all." He scooped up the photos. "I've got to get the front page reset. Be sure to give Accounting a voucher for these shots. Good work, Peter!" With a wave, Robbie headed for his office.

Leaving the editorial offices, Peter headed down to the newspaper's morgue, where copies of every *Daily Bugle* ever printed waited as a reference library for researchers and fact-checkers.

"I know I've seen those costumes somewhere before," Peter said to himself. "Maybe there's something in here."

He began looking for stories about the crimes Spider-Man had thwarted over the years. There were dozens. Hundreds—along with hundreds of editorials by *Bugle* publisher J. Jonah Jameson decrying the way the vigilante Spider-Man thwarted justice, obstructed authorities, ignored the law, destroyed private property, and allowed lawbreakers to escape. JJJ's pen was particularly acidic whenever Spider-Man failed. Reading those stories was enough to make Peter flinch.

Peter dropped the first stack of papers back at the reference desk and picked up the next.

And there, under the headline SPIDER-MAN FAILS AGAIN, was a photo of a collection of thugs being led into captivity by the police.

"Police Round up Suspects, While Spider-

Man Lets Boss Go Free," read the story's sub-head. Peter remembered that adventure. His aunt, May Parker, had been seriously ill, he'd just started as a student at ESU, and then a super-villain calling himself the "Master Planner" had hired a gang of plug-uglies and dressed them in . . .

"Bingo," Peter said aloud. "Those suits with the built-in gas masks. The colors are different, but they're the same kind that the Master Planner's men wore."

Peter knew that the Master Planner also had a secret identity. And he knew who it was—Doctor Otto Octavius. Doc Ock was back.

Peter wondered briefly if he ought to tell Captain America what he'd figured out.

"Not yet," he told himself. "Not until I'm sure."

Peter left the *Daily Bugle* building and resumed his guise as Spider-Man. He needed to get out and start looking for Ock.

At that moment, Doc Ock was briefing another of his minions by way of a viewscreen. Like Scudder, Rusty and Deason before him, this man was standing before the viewscreen and, like them, he did not dare to sit.

In all other ways, this man was unlike the

hired thugs of the evening before. Instead of coveralls and SCUBA gear, he wore a business suit cut in the European fashion, and wire-rimmed glasses. His thin hair was combed across the bald spot on the top of his head. By his outward appearance he might have been a successful businessman, a stockbroker or banker, perhaps. It was possible that he was a government minister.

Right now a thin film of sweat made his face shine, although the air was cool. The viewscreen before which he stood was located in a rustic cabin set among high mountains. Snow glistened from the distant peaks, and crisp alpine air brought the scent of pine needles into the cabin. But all of his attention was focused on the man with the adamantium tentacles who looked out at him from the high-tech apparatus.

"You have done well," Ock said, "in getting the nuclear material to Latveria. Doom is the one man on all the earth whose ambition matches my own. That makes him a threat . . . one that must be eliminated. Is there anything, however slight, that he lacks to have created an effective missile program?"

"Nothing, Doctor Octavius," replied the man with whom Doc Ock was conversing. "He has had adequate help when it looked like his program was going to bog down, yet nothing was made too easy for him and his scientists. Given the level of expertise Doom possesses, it was a foregone conclusion that he would achieve complete success on the theoretical end. From there, it was simply a matter of making the needed materials accessible."

"Excellent."

The man cleared his throat tentatively. "Doctor Doom is only awaiting the final shipment of American military hardware."

"And he will get it, never fear," Doc Ock said. "Yes, he'll get it. But perhaps not quite in the form he is anticipating."

"Do you have any orders for me, then?" the man asked.

"Yes. Begin circulating rumors of an imminent attack on Latveria—enough rumors for Doom to hear them, but not so many that the Western security organizations become alarmed and seek to root out their origins."

"I hesitate to ask, Doctor," the man said, "but my reward?"

"Your reward shall be everything that you deserve," Doc Ock replied.

"And my family?"

"Returned unharmed, just as I promised.

You shall see, your wages will be more than you expected."

"Thank you, Doctor."

"Don't thank me yet," Doc Ock said. "Do your job. At this moment, of all others, *you* must not fail in the slightest degree."

"I shall not fail."

Doc Ock did not reply. Instead, the viewscreen filled with swirling color and then went blank.

The businessman turned away, left the chalet, and entered his car. It was an expensive one. But today he had not been driven by his chauffeur, and the road back to the Latverian capital was long.

In his lair, Doctor Octopus smiled to himself. He was pleased. He had been able to turn one of Doom's officials into a spy. Of course, he'd had to kidnap the man's family. But that's why he was so certain the man would never double-cross him.

"*Your reward shall be everything that you deserve,*" Doc Ock replied.

6

Night had fallen over New York City, but the sounds and activity of Manhattan never stop. The blazing lights of Times Square, the screech of subways rounding curves, the blaring horns, the spotlights illuminating the Empire State Building, the aircraft warning lights flashing red from the top of the World Trade Center, the ships' horns from the harbor—it was all part of the cacophony that made New York the bustling heart of world commerce.

And high above it all, Spider-Man swung by a thread, on the lookout for anything unusual in the streets of the city he had taken into his special care.

The uncanny feeling that warned him of

danger—his spider-sense—had been quiet all day as he restlessly patrolled the concrete canyons. Now that sense began tingling with thrilling urgency.

Spidey altered course to head for the source of the feeling. Traffic moved below him on one of the cross streets that ran east-west on the island of Manhattan. Here in the middle of downtown that traffic was slow, progressing from light to light at a stately pace punctuated by car horns, shouts, and expressive gestures.

Spider-Man soon found the source of the warning: a panel truck stuck in traffic behind a delivery van double-parked in the middle of a block. Spidey came to rest on a wall nearby, holding onto the rough surface with the tips of his fingers and toes. He watched as the panel truck, with the words "World Wide Imports" stenciled on the side, inched slowly up over the curb in order to get around the blocking mass of the delivery van.

"There's never a traffic cop around when you need one," Spidey mused. "I suppose I could give them a citizen's citation, but it'll be more fun to find out where they're going and what they're up to."

By now the panel truck had finished its maneuver and was once again heading east.

Spider-Man launched himself into the air, trusting his spider-sense and his long-practiced ability at web-slinging to find places for his web-lines. He followed the truck with ease, sometimes swinging above it, sometimes behind, but never letting it get out of sight.

"Maybe the three guys I missed last night will be aboard," he said. "It would be a pleasure to ask them where they ran off to." He had no way of knowing exactly who was in the van. Still, his spider-sense told him these were not good people, and his instincts told him they were somehow connected to the previous night's events.

The truck was headed for the Queensborough Bridge, heading out to Long Island. Spidey stayed with it. He used first the bridge's massive supporting columns, then the elevated subway tracks on the Queens end of the bridge to attach his webs, and swung along in swift pursuit.

The truck wound its way through narrow cobblestoned sidestreets leading toward an entrance ramp for the Brooklyn-Queens Expressway. For the first time, Spider-Man began to have difficulty finding places to attach his web-lines.

The truck shot up the ramp and merged with the swiftly-moving traffic that flowed east along the expressway. Having run out of places on which to anchor a web-line, Spidey landed on the roof of a delivery van traveling a few car-lengths behind the truck he pursued.

"Lead on, MacDuff," he murmured, as though speaking to the truck's driver. "You have my undivided attention."

A few miles later, Spidey spotted the truck's turn signal blinking. He looked ahead to a large metal sign suspended above the roadway. The sign read "Long Island Expressway—Next Right." The truck switched lanes and barreled up the entry lane to the expressway.

"Looks like this is my stop," said Spidey, shooting a web-line to the road sign. Pushing off from the delivery van, he swung high above the flow of traffic, coming to rest on the roof of an eighteen-wheel tractor-trailer traveling behind the panel truck.

Perched on the trailer, Spidey watched as the panel truck switched lanes to allow the eighteen-wheeler to pass. The larger vehicle accelerated and matched speed with the truck.

"It's like having door-to-door service," said Spidey, grinning under his mask. Creeping over to the edge of the trailer, he jumped.

While still in the air, Spider-Man fired both of his web-shooters, creating a soft cushion on the panel truck's roof. This allowed him to land softly. No one inside the truck felt or heard his arrival. With his position secure, he lay back on the top of the vehicle, crossed his arms behind his head, and watched the stars go by above, far beyond the sodium-vapor lights of the Long Island Expressway.

I should have thought of this earlier, he told himself. This is definitely the way to follow a car.

The truck swerved, slowed, and turned another corner.

Rest time's over, Spidey thought. Get ready for playtime.

He sat up and faced forward. The panel truck was entering a parking lot at an industrial building. The sign over the gate read "Millstone Electronics Products." A smaller sign below it warned that unauthorized personnel were strictly forbidden to enter.

A guard shack stood beside the gate, but the guard was lying on his side, halfway out of the shack, while three black-clad men rolled the chain-link gate open and waved the truck in. The three were dressed identically to those from the previous night. Spider-Man allowed himself a small chuckle. His instincts—and spider-sense—had been correct. These men worked for Doctor Octopus.

Spidey rolled off the far side of the truck from the men on the ground, where he wouldn't be seen, and shot a web-line up to the side of a water tower on the top of the factory building. Moments later, he was on the roof, hidden from view. Down below, the lock on the front door of the factory building vanished in a blue-white, silent flash.

Flashlight beams flickered inside the building. The bad guys, whoever they might be, were already hard at work.

But I'll bet you aren't expecting a visit from your friendly neighborhood Spider-Man, the web-slinger thought. Let's see what you're after.

Crawling down the side of the building, he pushed open a window on the top floor and rolled through. He moved along the ceiling to the top of a two-story atrium above the entrance doors. The team that had entered the factory was returning, pushing a crate on a hand cart before them.

"Got 'em?" called out one of the men who had waited at the door.

"Yeah."

"Good. We're thirty-five seconds ahead of schedule."

"Time to join the party," Spidey said, and loosened his grip.

He landed feet first on the man who was pushing the cart. The man smashed into the floor, groaned once, and lay still.

"Excuse me," Spider-Man said to the black-clad intruders. "Is this where I get the bus to Ryker's Island prison?"

"I'll give you a bus," said another of the group of thieves. He swung a length of pipe at Spider-Man's head. Spidey leaped over the blow, twisted in mid-air, and shot a web-line to the end of the makeshift club. The other end of the web he attached to a pillar. When the line tightened, the man's own momentum pulled him over onto his back.

"Gee, I'm sorry," Spidey said. "That looked like it hurt."

A tingle from his spider-sense made Spider-Man drop to the floor and roll. The high-intensity light of the laser the criminals had used to burn open the filing cabinets flashed through the air over Spidey's head. The wall behind him turned into a smoking pit where the blast hit.

Rolling to his feet, Spidey spotted the thug carrying the laser. "Hey!" he yelled. "Didn't your mom tell you that you could put your eye out playing with that thing?"

Spider-Man launched a web-line upward and swung around to smash into the man's arm, forcing him to drop the laser. Spidey dove for it, snatching it up before the weapon's recent owner could recover from the stunning blow.

Another tingle from his spider-sense. Spider-Man leapt aside as a burst of gunfire cut through the air where he'd just been standing. But as Spidey landed, a fine-mesh net of copper fell over him, launched from the bell-shaped muzzle of a handgun wielded by a black-clad thug just inside the door.

Spider-Man floundered, tangled in the copper mesh. Then the bottom of the net touched the floor, and a high-powered jolt of electricity flowed through the metal net to the ground. The blast of power coursed through Spider-Man's body, and he convulsed as his muscles contracted involuntarily.

"The boss said we might expect a visit from you," said the tallest man there. He rubbed his elbow where Spider-Man had struck him, then bent to recover the laser device. "So he gave us something to take you out."

He raised the laser and pointed it at Spider-Man's bound and paralyzed body. "Goodbye, wall-crawler."

Before the tall man could press the firing stud, the two men guarding the front door fell to the floor. The dull *thock!* made by their heads being knocked together still echoed through the room as a red, white and blue form jumped past them. Another motion, too fast for the eye to see, and a star-spangled shield flew from the newcomer's left arm to smash into the laser device.

Captain America had arrived.

The laser exploded in a shower of sparks. The man who had held it jumped back, grabbing his hand as the smashed weapon fell to the floor and burned.

Another of the thugs swung his fist at Captain America's jaw. The Avenger raised his hand and caught the fist squarely. Then Cap squeezed and twisted, bringing his assailant to his knees as the fist was bent back.

Two other men had picked up Captain America's shield from where it lay on the floor. Now they ran toward Cap, hoping to smash him with his own weapon.

Captain America saw them coming. He ran toward his assailants even as they ran toward him. At the last moment he launched himself into a handspring, flying forward feet first. The soles of his red boots smashed out in a vicious kick to the center of the round adamantium alloy shield. The two men behind it fell, stunned. Captain America picked up his shield and slid his left arm through its straps.

Captain America had arrived.

He spun about and raised the shield in front of him as yet another of the masked gangsters pulled out a pistol and fired two quick shots. The slugs bounced harmlessly off of the face of the shield. The man turned and fled, leaving the room empty except for Captain America, Spider-Man, and several unconscious thugs.

Cap went to Spider-Man's side and pulled the mesh away from him.

Spider-Man was cramped and stiff, nearly paralyzed. Captain America pulled him to his feet.

"Come on," Cap said, rubbing life back into Spider-Man's stiffened arms. "We have to get the rest of them."

From outside came a sudden burst of noise: first the roar of a truck's engine coming suddenly to life, and then the screech of tires as the vehicle pulled away.

"The crate," Spider-Man managed to gasp out.

Outside, they found the cart that had held the wooden box the criminals had come for. It was empty.

"**W**hat brought you here?" Captain America asked moments later, as the two super heroes stood outside the factory. Flashing lights approaching in the distance told them the police would be arriving soon.

"I followed the bad guys from Manhattan," Spider-Man said. His breathing was still shaky after his close encounter with forty thousand volts. He paused. "Why were *you* here?"

"Thought *they* would be."

"Another component for that Clementine rocket?"

Captain America nodded. "They were ready for you. After last night I suppose that's only to have been expected. Unfortunately, because that newspaper ran my picture today they were also ready for me. I wasn't able to prevent their getaway."

Spider-Man didn't mention how it was that the newspaper had run those photos, but he suddenly felt ashamed. I can't think beyond my grocery bill, he thought. And here's Captain America—if he ever thought about himself first instead of other people I haven't heard of it.

"How about the guard at the gate?" Spider-Man asked after a moment. "I saw he was down. Does he need first aid?"

"He's okay," Captain America said. "I already checked him. It was some sort of non-lethal knockout gas that got him. He's probably in better shape than you are right now."

"I know who's behind this series of crimes," Spidey said after another long pause. "At least I think I do."

"That'll help. I'm pretty sure there's a connection with Doctor Doom, but I haven't figured out exactly what it is or how it works. And there are some inconsistencies, some things that don't fit, in that picture."

"Okay," Spidey began. He was starting to get his strength back. That had been quite a jolt he'd taken. "A few years ago, I fought a group of criminals, over on the west side of Manhattan. They were involved in the theft of nuclear materials. That's one link with current events. The big link, though, was their uniforms. The same jumpsuits with the built-in gas masks. They were real big on using knock-out gas. That gang worked for someone called the Master Planner. But he's got another name, one that more people recognize: Doctor Octopus."

"The atomic research scientist gone wrong," Captain America said. "That makes sense. Do you think he's teaming up with Doom?"

"Not too likely. Last I heard, they hated each other's guts. But assuming I'm right, does that help you?"

"Not unless you can tell me where Octopus is right now."

"I wish I knew that," Spidey told him. "But I don't. That part they grabbed tonight, though—what was it?"

"A radar-based anti-tracker. It makes it impossible for anyone to get a lock on a Clementine, and impossible to get a fix on where it was fired from."

"What good does that do?"

"The theory," said Cap, "was that if we only had one working silo left, our enemies wouldn't be able to find out where that silo was."

The police cars arrived, accompanied by blaring sirens and a screech of brakes.

"I think we can turn things here over to the local constabulary now," Captain America said. "Do you feel well enough to travel?"

"I suppose," Spidey said. "Where are we going?"

"To Kansas or New Mexico," Cap said. "Those are the locations of the Clementine silos. Unless I miss my guess, that's where we'll find this gang next. I want to get there before they do."

Captain America walked over to one of the police officers. "The scene is yours," he said. "You'll find some members of the gang that broke in scattered around inside. Most of them are unconscious, but you should still consider them armed and dangerous." Reaching into his belt, Cap extracted a gray-toned business card and handed it to the officer. "This is the number for a Colonel Martin Barron—he's leading an investigation linked to this break-in. He'll need to interrogate the prisoners once they've been secured."

"Will you be staying to help us out?"

"I'm afraid that I can't, but I'll be glad to

drop by the station tomorrow to answer any questions you might have then," Captain America said. "If there is a tomorrow," he added quietly, under his breath, as he turned away.

Captain America was a veteran of World War II. He had seen for himself how dirty and ugly a global war could be, and he had no wish to see such a war repeated. All of the signs, though, suggested that someone who didn't share his opinions was trying to gain the means of mass destruction that could obliterate entire cities.

"If we hurry," he said to Spider-Man when he got back to the web-slinger, "we can get to the Clementine site before Octopus's people can get the radar disruptor there."

"How are we going to get there?" Spidey asked. "Ock's men have at least a half-hour lead on us."

"I can cut that down to nearly nothing," Captain America said. "Want a lift to the airport?"

"Sure thing."

Cap sprinted off into the night. A powerful roar reached Spidey's ears. Apparently, Cap had come to the crime scene by motorcycle. Soon he came wheeling out of the dark into the floodlit ground surrounding the factory.

Police and emergency medical technicians were already swarming over the building, but they stayed well clear of the two super heroes.

"Jump on and hold tight," Cap said. "We're in a hurry."

Spider-Man got up on the back of the motorcycle. Captain America put it into gear, fed gas to the throttle and sped off. Air rushed by Spider-Man's head.

I wonder how fast we're going, he thought as they flashed by a car on the highway. On second thought, I don't think I want to know.

Spider-Man looked around. He was reasonably familiar with landmarks in the Long Island area. "Hey!" he shouted, loud enough to be heard over the engine and the wind. "We aren't heading to any airport I know of!"

If Captain America responded, Spidey didn't hear it. All he could feel was the vibration of the engine. The lines on the road looked like dots flying past him only inches beneath his feet.

I swing from a web-line thousands of feet over Manhattan, he told himself. Why should I be nervous about a little speed on the open highway?

Fortunately, the ride lasted only a few minutes before they came to a field surrounded by a high fence. Cap revved the cycle, aimed for an embankment, and jumped the fence, standing on the pegs as the motorcycle flew across to land, still rolling at high speed across a grassy field.

Ahead of them, dimly reflecting the headlight's glow, Spider-Man could see the sleek shape of an Avengers' quinjet. Captain America brought the motorcycle to a skidding halt beside the aircraft's door.

"I was afraid that I'd have to go to Latveria in a hurry, so I brought some transportation," Cap explained. "It'll do to get us to the Midwest."

Spider-Man could only nod in agreement. The two heroes dismounted from the motorcycle. Captain America led the way aboard the jet and strapped himself into the pilot's seat on the right side of the cockpit.

"Get in and tie down," he said. "The ride may be a little bumpy at first."

"I'm putting my tray table in a fully upright and locked position," Spidey said. "Ready when you are. But shouldn't we have a destination in mind?"

"That's my next step," Captain America said. He fired up the powerful radio transmitters in the quinjet, and—using what Spider-

Man assumed were secret military frequencies—attempted to contact control at each of the Clementine silos. New Mexico answered up with all normal; Kansas didn't answer at all.

"Looks like Kansas is it," Spider-Man said.

"Then I say go," Cap replied. He switched on the powerful engines. They answered with a roar. "Brakes full on, flaps full down, fuel mix full rich."

A moment more and Cap pushed the throttle all the way forward. The quinjet trembled. "Brakes off," Cap said, and the jet leaped forward, going airborne almost instantly. Cap didn't slow down. He pulled back on the control yoke to gain altitude, and twisted left to point southwest.

"Next stop, Kansas," he said, and kicked in the afterburners.

Spider-Man felt himself being crushed back into the seat. "Wow. You sure have some acceleration on this thing."

"Tony Stark built it, not me," Captain America said. "He put a lot of little tricks and surprises into it. The quickest route to where we're going is a ballistic trajectory, so that's what we're taking."

"That's a sub-orbital hop," Spidey said. "Well, *I'm* impressed, anyhow."

Cap revved the cycle, aimed for an embankment, and jumped the fence . . .

He looked out of the cockpit windows. The stars were looking very big, very bright, and dead ahead. Looking forward and below, he thought he could see the horizon start to curve down on either end, as their altitude increased.

"Fifty miles up and climbing," Cap said after a few moments more of silence. "Cutting in the auxiliary rockets."

Another roar, and again Spider-Man felt acceleration pushing him back in his seat.

"Is there anything this jet won't do?" he asked.

"It won't turn into a monster truck, and it makes a lousy cup of coffee," Captain America said. "Other than that, not much." He busied himself with the navigational gear.

"Any plans on what we're going to do once we arrive?" Spidey asked a bit later.

"Survey the situation at hand, work with the troops, and do the best we can under the circumstances."

"In other words, fake it."

"Not exactly. But if it helps you to think of it that way . . . yes."

The flight continued. Spider-Man took the opportunity to fill his web-shooters. From his belt he removed cartridges of web-fluid, snapping the fresh containers into the watch band-like devices strapped to his wrists. The long swing from Manhattan to the Long Island site, on top of a full day of webbing around town, had lowered his reserves more than he liked.

"Coming in for a landing," Captain America said finally. "Look alert once we're out there on the ground. The problem could be anything. And these people may well be ordinary soldiers having communications problems. Mark them as friendly."

"As far as I'm concerned," Spidey said, " 'friendly' means 'not shooting at me.' And I hate to mention it, but *real* troops haven't been scoring too high lately on the Spider-scale either."

"In that case," said Captain America, "don't forget to duck. And follow my lead."

The quinjet reentered the atmosphere and flew on toward the Clementine launch area, which was located in an otherwise unremarkable flat area of Kansas. On the ground below the jet, cornfields stretched out toward the horizon in every direction. The night was dark, the full moon washing the landscape with its bluish white light. Here and there the lights of an isolated farmhouse glittered.

"Is there any way to see what we're getting

into before we land?" Spidey asked after a few minutes.

Cap turned on a set of screens mounted on the control panel. "Forward viewers on full magnification. We have some good optics here. Take a look when the site comes over the horizon." He dialed in some numbers. "Latitude and longitude punched in. We'll have a lock in a bit."

At the speed the quinjet was making, the missile site was soon on the viewer. High-security lights blazed white light down on the chain link and razor wire fences, the roads, the guard towers.

"Anything?"

"Nothing on the ground yet," Spidey said. "Wait a minute—I've got movement. Watch it, Cap—black suits!"

"I have them," Captain America said. "Looks like Octopus's people are already in possession of the site. We have to assume they have the Clementine go-codes. Ready to roll in hot?"

The screen wasn't the only way to see the missile site now. The brightly lit area was clearly visible from the cockpit windows.

"Ready for anything you are," Spidey said.

"I'm going to put us down on that east-west service road. Our target is the control room, to prevent launch. Once that area is secured, we'll apprehend the rest of the men outside."

"If Doc Ock is there, I'd like to be the one to take him out," Spider-Man said. "Sort of a long-standing grudge, you might say."

"Fair enough," Cap said. "I'm going to pop the hatches the second we stop rolling. I'm marking the control room on your screen. Get ready to go."

The quinjet swooped low, barely clearing the fence as Captain America brought it in. He flared the nose and cut power to put the aircraft on the deck fast.

"Engine thrust reverse full, brakes set. Airspeed two hundred. One hundred. Fifty. Go!"

Cap punched a switch on the instrument board. The sides of the cockpit fell away leaving nothing but the hot, dusty night outside. Spider-Man rolled out of the jet on his side, hit the ground, rolled again, and looked up, trying to make out a landmark to recognize the control bunker. Behind him, he heard the doors of the quinjet cycle shut.

High on the nearest guard tower, one of the black-garbed minions of Doctor Octopus slewed his searchlight toward the newly arrived aircraft. Spidey shot a web-line to the top of a light pole and launched himself into the air, swinging out of the cone of light. An alarm began to sound, its shrill tone echoing through the night.

Another black-suit trotted by, holding a rifle in his hands. He was intent on the quinjet and never noticed Spidey swinging past him until a web-line caught him around the legs, tripping him. Then Spider-Man changed direction again, with a web attached to the bottom of a guard tower. He had the control bunker in sight.

Off to his left an automatic rifle opened up, firing bursts of two, then three shots. None of them came near Spidey. The rifle stopped abruptly, then opened up again, this time in a long, ripping burst to empty the magazine. The muzzle flashes were aimed in the opposite direction now—Captain America was at work.

Spider-Man made one long swing and let go of his line. He flew through the air, tucked, and landed on his feet at the door to the command bunker. Two guards stood with rifles pointed nervously toward the outer darkness. Spidey brought down the one on the right with a powerful kick to the midsection. Before the man's companion could react, Spidey launched a punch to the jaw that knocked him back, staggering, against the concrete wall of the command bunker. The man slumped to the ground, his rifle falling from nerveless fingers.

Spidey gripped the door by the handle and hinges. "Whoever built this place didn't count on a visit from someone with the proportionate strength of a spider!" He twisted, pulled, and the door tore away from its hinges. The space beyond was lit by red light, and it was crowded with black-suited thugs.

Spider-Man waded in, fists and feet smashing his opponents. They fought back. A blow creased Spider-Man's jaw, making him see stars. Then the stars were there in person as Captain America joined the fray.

"What kept you?" Spidey called to his companion.

"I had to run," Cap replied. He punched out with his shield rim and knocked the nearest black-suit to the floor. "Not everyone can swing on his own trapeze."

Over against the far wall, two men stationed thirty feet apart simultaneously twisted identical keys in identical locks.

"System armed," a synthesized, recorded voice announced over hidden loudspeakers. It sounded unnaturally calm and clear amid the mayhem.

"No time to lose!" Cap shouted—and if he had been fighting before, it was nothing to what Spidey saw now. The Avenger looked like a double-feature of kung-fu movies as he kicked and punched his way across the floor toward the control panel.

Time to take the high road, thought Spidey.

He leapt to the ceiling and started crawling across it above the heads of the combatants. From his upside-down position he could see a glowing button on the control panel. A man reached out toward the button. With split-second reflexes Spidey shot a web-line to the man's shoulder, pulling him down and away. Another man rushed in to take his place.

Spider-Man threw a web at the newcomer as well, but the line tangled as one of the black-suits unexpectedly ran forward, momentarily blocking Spidey's line of sight. When he could see the button again it was no longer flashing. Now it burned with a steady glow.

"Primary launch sequence initialized," the loudspeaker announced. Spidey saw Captain America push forward even harder through the surging mass of villains on the floor below, clearing a pathway with fists and feet—but the control panel was still out of the Avenger's reach. "Ten second standby. Nine. Eight. Seven . . ."

Just let me get to the keys, Spidey thought. Let me get there in time.

He swooped down, using the momentum

of his swing to smash his way forward through the press of bodies. His foes tumbled out of the way. Sounds of combat filled the air: heavy breathing, the slap of flesh against flesh, cries of pain, shouts of exertion—and above all, the mechanical voice counting down, "Three, two, one . . ."

Spider-Man reached the key on the left-hand side of the panel. He pulled away the unconscious body of the man who had turned the key in its lock, and reached out to twist it back. The lock snapped back to Unarmed—but the synthesized voice wasn't counting any longer. It was saying something new.

"Missile armed. Engage primary launch system. Missile away."

Abruptly the room fell silent.

"No!" Spider-Man shouted. His face was wet under his mask; he couldn't tell if it was from sweat or from tears. "You saw it. We got so close—"

"I know," Captain America said. Aside from Spidey, Cap was now the only person still standing in the room. "We still have things to do. Come on!"

The two super heroes dashed from the control bunker just as a roaring sound filled the sky. From out of the ground a pillar of fire rose into the night. Atop the fire and amid the smoke Spidey could make out the silvery shape of the Clementine missile.

"There's nothing more you could have done," Captain America said. "But we haven't lost yet. Right now, we need to find out what happened to the troops stationed here. After that, we can get back to the quinjet."

Still, Spider-Man couldn't help blaming himself. If only he hadn't taken so much time to recover at the factory on Long Island, they could have reached the missile site five minutes earlier. Even one minute earlier might have been enough. Or maybe if he hadn't taken the time to web that one black-suit on the way over to the bunker. Was that move what had cost him the seconds—seconds were all he would have needed—in which he could have saved civilization from the beginning of a global war?

A quick search of the base turned up the missing soldiers. The black-garbed thugs had overpowered them with knock-out gas and locked them in a supply shed.

"Well, at least *something* went right," muttered Spider-Man. He breathed a sigh of relief. At least no real harm had come to the soldiers.

Suddenly, Spider-Man felt a strong charge

running through his body. His spider-sense was tingling like crazy. He spun around, seeking the source. Then he looked up.

A blossom of light appeared in the sky.

"Get down! Cover your eyes!" Captain America shouted.

The sky above the launch site exploded in a pulsing globe of colors as, high overhead in the boundary regions of near space, the nuclear warhead of the Clementine missile exploded.

The searchlights in the towers flared up and died in a shower of sparks. The sounds of engines, the hum of compressors, all died at the same moment. The light in the sky changed from brilliant white to dull red shot through with black, and faded to a glowing patch slightly lighter against the stars.

"Hey!" Spider-Man said in the silence after the light in the sky had faded. "I thought that rocket wasn't supposed to have a self-destruct on it."

"It doesn't," Captain America replied. "Let's go find out what's happened. Get back to the quinjet the fastest way you can."

Moving quickly and without comment, Spidey shot a web-line up to a pole where a now-burned-out light had flared only a moment before, and swung out from it.

A blossom of light appeared in the sky.

The pale moonlight showed the quinjet waiting on the roadway. Spider-Man got there ahead of Captain America, reached for the opening button on the side door, and pushed it. The door didn't open.

Captain America arrived a few seconds later. He was breathing heavily after the hard fight and a fast run. Spidey gestured at the door.

"Can't get in."

"Not surprising," Cap replied. "What do you know about EMPs?"

Quite a bit, Spider-Man told himself. As a physics student, Peter Parker could hardly avoid knowing about it. But telling Cap how much he knew might blow his cover and reveal his secret identity.

"EMP stands for electromagnetic pulse," Spidey said. That much knowledge, at least, was probably safe for him to reveal. If anything was safe, now. "What about it?"

Captain America opened a panel on the side of the quinjet and pulled out a lever. "Emergency opening system," he said. "An EMP is a huge dose of energy. When you have a nuke explode high enough, but not too high, it sends a broad-band blast of energy in every direction."

Cap pulled on the lever and a mechanical

latch snicked open. He pushed on the door and turned it on its hinges, opening it manually. He then entered the aircraft.

"That electromagnetic pulse," Cap went on, as Spider-Man followed him forward to the cockpit, "will induce a voltage in anything that can conduct electricity. Enough voltage to overload and burn out all sorts of electronic and electrical gear. Tony Stark has hardened the quinjet against most EMP effects, although it looks like we've lost some of the auxiliaries. We'll see in a minute if the emergency systems are still working."

Captain America reached the pilot's seat and turned a switch mounted under a safety case on the panel. A faint red glow answered him, filling the cockpit with light.

"Good. Tony's work held. Let's see what the situation is out there in the world. Depending on the altitude and the location of the EMP, things could be very bad indeed."

For a few minutes Captain America worked at the control panel, opening metal shutters that hid screens now filling with data.

"I have a location and altitude on the explosion," he said at last. "The EMP blanketed everything from Alaska to central Europe. Essentially, any electronic or electrical device or system that was in use in the western hemisphere has just been put out of commission."

"A layer of water would shield the effects, wouldn't it?" Spider-Man said.

"That's right."

"When I first encountered Ock posing as the Master Planner, he had his headquarters under water," Spidey remembered. "I'll bet that's where his new headquarters is located."

"Probably," Cap agreed. "We know that the Master Planner's thugs have been stealing material to create nuclear weapons. We also know that the Planner is really Octopus, through your earlier run-in with him. Finally, we know that Octopus thinks big. If you plan to play with fire, you put on an asbestos suit. If you're playing with nuclear missiles, it makes sense to take precautions against nuclear explosions."

"I'll bet," Spidey said, "that right now those goons of his are coming up out of underwater bases in New York harbor, San Francisco Bay, Lake Michigan, Lake Maracaibo, and every other body of water near a major city in this hemisphere. They've probably got the only working radios, the only working computers . . ."

"Octopus has no respect for human life," Cap said harshly. "Think about it. Every heart pacemaker, every hospital machine, all the navigational gear and radios and radar and controls on every ship at sea and every aircraft in the air . . . they all stopped working when that Clementine missile detonated."

Spidey didn't want to think about it. Not right now. Maybe later, when there wasn't anything else left that a Spider-Man could do. He drew a deep breath. "Tell me, do *we* have a working aircraft?"

"Yes. I believe we do."

"Then I think we'd better get going to the other Clementine site. Ock stole the codes for both of them, and he isn't the kind of man who'd settle for half a victory. Do you think he'll try to black out the other half of the world?"

"I don't know," Cap admitted. "But I think it's funny that the border of the EMP, the very edge of its effect, just happened to be on the border of Latveria. This scheme of his may be more complex than either of us suspect."

"That's what you get for not being a twisted criminal genius," Spider-Man told him. "You just can't predict what a lunatic like Ock will think of next."

"And you can?" Cap said as he fired up

the jets on the Avengers' aircraft and raised the quinjet into the air.

Spidey didn't answer. Outside the cockpit windows, from horizon to horizon the ground was dark. No lights from buildings, no headlights from cars. The world outside was empty of evidence of twentieth-century humanity.

Although the jet itself was operational, the automatic pilot had been disabled by the blast of electromagnetic energy. Cap was flying manually, one eye on the gyros, one on the cockpit windows. After a few more seconds of silence, the Avenger spoke again.

"But this time I think you're right. Our next stop should be New Mexico, to make sure that the second Clementine rocket never launches."

CHAPTER
—9—

"**O**kay, I know a little bit about how launch codes work," Spider-Man confessed. "The go-codes that Ock stole won't launch a missile by themselves. So where is the other half kept? The part that the missile has to match in order to launch?"

"When Ock punches the go-codes into Clementine, they're matched against a set of codes kept on a dark satellite in orbit," Cap replied.

"Cap!" Spidey said. "This quinjet can make orbital burns. What's to stop us from going to that satellite and changing the codes? We could disable the second Clementine."

"I think you were right the first time and we should go to the site," Cap replied. "It was in friendly hands last time we heard from it. If we're fast we can keep it that way, without having to disable anything."

"We can split up," Spider-Man argued. "I'll go change the codes, and that way it won't matter what happens on the ground. Meanwhile, you can try talking the people on the ground into disabling their rocket, so it won't matter what happens in space."

Cap shook his head. "That'll never work. I'm the one who knows where the satellite is, and I'm the one who knows how to fly this aircraft. I'll have to go up, while you stay on the ground and talk the United States Army into shutting down their own bird."

"I hate to tell you this, Cap, but I've got a lousy track record for talking the authorities into *anything*."

"I have every confidence in you," Cap said. "We're coming up on the New Mexico site. Time for you to get off the bus. I'll meet with you back here as soon as possible."

Spider-Man sighed. "Right."

A small airfield serviced the hidden Clementine base. Captain America quickly put the quinjet down on the tarmac, and Spider-Man jumped out and ran for cover on the side of the strip. The quinjet's engines rose again to a roar and the vehicle streaked into the air.

It turned to the south, and glittered in the moonlight for a few seconds before fading from view.

"Okay," Spidey said. "Time to put on my friendliest smile and explain to a bunch of soldiers who just watched the beginnings of World War III that they shouldn't shoot me first and ask questions later."

The base lay just past an earthen berm, little more than a mound of dirt piled between the fence and the airstrip. Everything was dark and silent. The EMP had burned out this base's generators and lights as well, leaving nothing but the anxious eyes of soldiers staring into the dark to detect an approaching enemy.

They'll be wearing night-vision goggles, Spidey thought. I'll keep to the shadows until I see what these guys are wearing. If it's black jumpsuits, I could be in line for some more exercise.

Cautiously, he made his way toward the gate. The soldiers on guard were wearing US Army uniforms.

So far, so good, Spidey thought. The gang's all here. Let me get to their commanding officer and I can tell him what's going on.

Meanwhile, Captain America was nosing the Avengers' quinjet upward through the stratosphere. The satellite with the Clementine go-codes was hardened to withstand an EMP. After all, the entire system had been designed for use after the start of a nuclear war. And the satellite was a dark one, which meant it was designed to be hard to spot. Stealth technology kept it off radar, and limited its electromagnetic signature so that radio frequency direction finders wouldn't be able to get a fix on it.

Still, with his security clearances, Cap knew the general area where the satellite was likely to be, he knew what it looked like, and, most important, he knew how to make it initiate a broadcast. If he sent it a signal like the Clementine missile's onboard computer requesting launch authorization, the satellite would respond by sending a permission signal.

From this altitude the earth lay spread out below the quinjet. The western hemisphere was in the shadow of night. Where usually the cities would glisten like diamond shards, nothing showed. No lights revealed the location of Boston, Washington, St. Louis, New Orleans, San Diego, or Los Angeles. Toronto and Mexico City were blacked out. Portland was dark, as was Minneapolis and Detroit. Nothing showed from below. It was a sight that no one had ever seen from an aircraft before. Electricity had come to the cities before the first transcontinental flights began.

Cap set the one working radio on the quinjet to scanning for broadcasts from below. Again silence greeted him. Every radio and television station was off the air. Not even military broadcasts broke the crackle of static. The EMP of Doc Ock's first nuke had wiped the electromagnetic spectrum clean. Cap turned his attention to finding the satellite before the same could happen to the rest of the earth. He cut in the rockets as the jets starved for oxygen in the high atmosphere, and continued climbing.

In New Mexico, Spider-Man approached the gate of the missile site.

"Halt, who goes there?" came a shout from the guard house.

Wow, Spidey thought. They really *do* say that.

"Spider-Man," the wall-crawler replied. "I'm on your side."

"Spider-Man?" replied the voice. "I was told to expect you. Please come this way."

They expected *me*? Spidey thought. I didn't know I was coming here myself. He stepped forward. Suddenly he felt a jolt. His spider-sense was sending him a warning.

"The commanding officer wants to talk with you, pronto," the soldier said, as he came out of the night to meet Spidey. "He said to treat you special."

The tingling from Spider-Man's warning sense increased. "Is it just me," he asked the guard, "or does that sound suspicious to you, too?"

Another soldier approached. This one was a very tall man indeed. "Yeah," he said. "But don't worry. Last time I saw you was in New York, and I didn't have a chance to deal with you properly then."

The man shot out a fist to hit Spider-Man in the face. But Spidey had been warned. He ducked beneath the blow, then punched upward.

"Were you at the factory, or were you at the roadblock?" Spidey asked as the man groaned under the impact. "Not that it matters."

Another thought came to the wall-crawler: suppose these were men from the squad who had fired on him at ESU? In that case, they really *were* soldiers, and he shouldn't hurt them.

Another soldier was approaching from the rear. Spider-Man kicked backward, then leapt over the falling man. Two quick web-shots and the men were bound. But more were coming, their faces shining with sweat in the hot night, the light of the moon providing the only illumination. Spider-Man hit them as gently as possible, under the circumstances.

"I want to talk with your commanding officer," he said again. "This is all a mistake."

"No mistake," came another voice. An adamantium tentacle smashed into Spider-Man from behind, bringing him to his knees.

"Doc Ock!" Spidey exclaimed. "Finally. You don't know how tired I've gotten of playing hide-and-go-seek with you."

"This time, Spider-Man, the game is *tag, you're out.*"

Ock windmilled his tentacle arms so that they seemed to come from all directions at once, and smashed again and again at Spider-Man. And as if at some unspoken command, all the lights on the base came on at once.

"While the rest of the country is wrapped in fear in the dark," Ock sneered between blows, "I took precautions. I've been here for over a week now, waiting, preparing the final attack. This time I have won. This time you have no possible chance at inconveniencing me, let alone thwarting my plans. But, because you are an old and dear 'friend' I will allow you to see my triumph—from very close, indeed. The end is near, and at last I shall be the ruler of the world!"

"You're insane, Octopus," Spidey said, twisting to avoid Doc Ock's arms. If only he could get close enough. Doc Ock was an ordinary man, once you forgot about the metal tentacles controlled directly by his brain waves. Just a single punch to the jaw would take him out of the fight.

"Insane? Spider-Man, I'd thought better of you. Your taunting has been so much wittier in the past. But perhaps that's because in the past you've had a chance, however slight, of winning. This time, the victory is mine."

"One thing I've been wondering," Spidey said, jumping to avoid a sudden spearing attack from one of Doc Ock's extensible arms. "After you've blacked out the world, what will you do then? There's no long-term victory. The effects of the EMP will only last so long."

"That's where you're wrong," Octopus said. Two of his tentacles caught Spider-Man in a crushing embrace, pinning the super hero's arms to his sides, while a third held his legs, and the fourth one wrapped around Spidey's neck. "I don't have one weapon, I have many. As you shall shortly see."

*   *   *

Two of his tentacles caught Spider-Man in a crushing embrace . . .

As Spider-Man slowly slipped from consciousness on the sands of New Mexico, caught in Doc Ock's implacable stranglehold, high above the earth Captain America eased the quinjet into a matching orbit with a secret military satellite.

The satellite was the control system for the Clementine rocket, all right. Cap recognized it from the drawings he'd studied during the mission briefing for this case. Hard to believe that fewer than two full days had elapsed since he'd been informed of the break-in at the university, and the president had requested his help.

Now he floated in zero gravity high above the earth, ready to shut down America's final defense system, a system that had been subverted by a super-villain for his own nefarious ends.

All I have to do, Cap said to himself, is get over there, open the maintenance hatch on the top, and dial in new codes. There's a pressure suit in the emergency supplies storage on board, with fifteen minutes of air. Not a lot, but more than enough for this mission.

He unstrapped and headed back to don the suit. A few minutes later and he was ready to go. By depressurizing the aft cargo area he could turn that part of the quinjet into a crude airlock, so there would be air in the cockpit on his return from his spacewalk, and he'd have something to breathe on the way home. He looked around the cargo bay. What was left to take?

He spotted his shield floating nearby. He'd worn it back into the cargo bay.

I probably won't need it, he said to himself. It's just extra mass to maneuver with in zero gee.

But he had to admit that he'd be a lot more comfortable wearing his shield. He loosened the shield's straps to their maximum extent so that it would fit over the bulky pressure suit, then slid his left arm through the straps. Once the shield was in place, he pulled the lever that opened the outer door of the cargo bay.

The stars glittered impossibly bright outside the opening. Cap carefully climbed out. The magnetized soles of his spacesuit boots allowed him to stand on the quinjet's steel exterior without floating off. Then he unreeled the coil of safety cord that tied him to the main body of the quinjet. The satellite hovered above him, motionless against the star field beyond. Cap put his boots against the side of the quinjet and pushed off toward the satellite.

As he approached the satellite he saw that it was covered with some nozzle-like protuberances. Must be for steering the satellite in orbit, Cap thought. Then he saw that they were moving. Slowly the nozzles pointed toward him. *This wasn't in the briefing.*

Then a beam of green light lanced out of one of the nozzles. Those weren't maneuvering rockets at all, he realized. These were high-intensity lasers, part of the satellite's final defense against sabotage or attack.

Cap jerked sharply on his safety line, tumbling himself out of the path of the laser rays. As soon as Cap moved outside of their defensive sphere, the lasers shut off.

This presents a problem, Cap said to himself. I have to get inside the range of those lasers, go right up to the satellite, change the codes, and get back to the jet. And I have to do it in thirteen minutes.

Before my air runs out.

CHAPTER
—10—

"**S**pider-Man, can you hear me?"

"I hear you fine, Ock," Spidey said. He shook his head to clear it and looked around. He was in the base of a missile silo, chained to the wall. He tested his bonds. They were strong.

"How pleasant to have a chance to chat with you, without your trying to brain me while we talk," Octopus purred. "Did you ever wonder about the complexities of mankind? As long as you're here I thought we might expand a bit on the entire theory."

Doc Ock's voice came into the silo though hidden speakers. Spider-Man looked to his right, as far as the chains would allow him. The view ahead was blocked by a missile. He had seen one like it only a short time before, rising on a tail of fire.

Clementine.

To Spidey's right was a flat projection screen. On it he could see Doc Ock, standing in what looked like a control station. "As we travel along our paths in life," Ock continued, "many times we come to decision points that will alter the course of our entire journey. Some might take the easy road, others may take the hard one. That is where you and I come in. Believe it or not, we two are the same. We both chose a difficult path toward acceptance by the people of the world. I, with the corruption and eventual control of government. And you, with the everlasting vigilante work of either a madman or a true super hero. Define it as you will. However, though we are alike, our paths cross in irreversible collisions. Now you see why I must kill you. A pity really, considering what a great team we would have made. Would you reconsider joining me?"

"Octopus," said Spider-Man, "you have *got* to be kidding."

"I thought as much. That is a real pity. Behind me you can see my minions. They are busily setting the codes that will send the rocket you see on its way. They are adjusting the last details in its destination heading. They are arming its warhead. When they are done with these last few steps, I alone—with my arms of more than mortal reach—will turn the keys to arm the system, and I alone will press the button to commence the launch."

"You won't get away with this," Spidey said. He pulled on his left hand, the one out of sight—he hoped—from the viewscreens. The chain felt a little weaker there. Doc Ock had never fully appreciated what astounding strength Spider-Man had. Spidey hoped that Ock had underestimated it one last time.

"Yes, I will."

"With just one warhead? That's nowhere near enough."

"But I don't have just one warhead. I have dozens. They're located in Latveria. For months I have been feeding Doctor Doom's paranoia, while at the same time I have been anonymously aiding him with Latveria's nuclear program. Now that the western world has fallen silent, Doom will see it as the final preparation for an attack against him.

"And when a nuclear-tipped rocket, its origin untraceable, comes tumbling out of the sky to strike near, but not in, the Latverian capital, Doom will respond by attacking wildly in all directions. No one, thanks to my electronic blackout, will be able to talk with him. They will only be able to counter-attack. Latveria cannot take on the entire world; in the end, Doom will lose.

"But the world will have been reduced to rubble by then. And from the rubble I will emerge, with my technology intact and waiting, as mankind's savior. The nations of the world will come to me. They will have no choice. All power, all protection, all medicine, all communications, will be under my exclusive control. No one will be able to buy or sell unless I have given them permission. At last my dreams will have been fulfilled. I shall rule the world!"

"Delusions of grandeur," Spidey said. "You know, Ock, a few years of intensive professional care with a dozen psychiatrists could have you working almost as good as new."

Spider-Man's left hand was slipping out of the chain that bound it. After that, all he had to worry about was his right hand, his legs, his waist . . . and about what the fire of a rocket blast would do to a nearby Spider-Man, if Doc Ock launched before he was all the way free.

High above the earth, in orbit, Captain America had problems of his own. The lasers kept him from approaching the satellite, and his air was getting low.

Well, he said to himself, I certainly hope Spider-Man is having an easier time accomplishing *his* goal.

Refusing to back down, Cap reviewed the situation. The lasers were the problem. But the more he thought about it, he realized that they could be the solution as well. The military satellite was far larger than any communications satellite. It was twenty-five feet high and about fifteen feet in diameter. There were five laser turrets mounted evenly around it.

If Cap could put one of the lasers out of commission, he would have a six-foot wide window without any laser fire in which to approach the satellite head-on. His glistening adamantium alloy shield was his only hope. It had pulled him through close scrapes before, but never had the fate of the entire world rested upon its performance.

It was all a matter of figuring the angles, momentum, and minimal necessary force. Something a pool player does automatically while lining up a shot on a pool table. What made it more complicated for Captain America was the absence of gravity. That, and the fact that if he miscalculated he would be hit by a laser weapon, which would rupture the integrity of his suit and cause him to explosively decompress. Of course, there was one other difference. A pool table is stationary. The satellite was not—it rotated on its axis just as every large orbiting body does.

Cap checked a gauge on his spacesuit, saw that he had a little over five minutes more of air. Moving as quickly as the situation would allow, Cap pulled himself back on the tether until he was once again standing on the outer skin of the quinjet. He figured the angles as best he could, and pushed off.

Cap planned to use his shield to reflect a laser shot right back at one of the turrets. But it couldn't be the one that had fired the laser beam, for that turret would be at the back of the satellite by the time Cap got there.

As he entered the satellite's defensive sphere, the lasers began targeting him. His shield protected him, sending the deadly beams flying off harmlessly into space. He closed in on the satellite.

Taking careful aim, Cap chose the turret he wanted to hit. It was just coming around into his view, as the satellite slowly turned. Cap readjusted the angle at which he held the shield to the satellite and held his breath.

A laser shot hit the shield near its center, and bounced back at the satellite. A direct

A laser shot hit the shield near its center, and bounced back at the satellite.

hit! The laser turret he had targeted glowed and melted. Cap's momentum continued to carry him toward the satellite, which still fired at him with the remaining lasers.

Two yards from the satellite, one of the laser shots hit his tether, which was not entirely protected by his shield. The tether parted instantly. Cap now had a new problem. Without the tether, how could he stop himself? And how could he pull himself back to the quinjet?

Even as those questions popped into mind, Cap acted instinctively. He rotated his body around, so that his feet were now pointed at the satellite, and crouched down to present a smaller target to the still-firing lasers.

A second later he was past the point where the lasers could target him—he was too close to the satellite. His boots made contact with the satellite's metal shell . . . and held. Cap reached out with his arms and grabbed hold of plates projecting from the satellite's sides. Carefully avoiding the laser turrets, Cap crawled around part of the satellite until he spotted the access door he sought. All he had to do now was open it and change the go-code settings.

There it was, just ahead. He tried it. It was locked.

"Something else the briefings didn't mention," Cap said aloud. He only had a couple of minutes of air left.

Spider-Man was still chained to the wall, mere feet away from the base of the rocket. He'd managed to get a little slack when his left hand came free. He was careful to keep that hand out of sight from the viewscreen off his right shoulder.

Fortunately, Doc Ock wasn't watching him constantly. The bespectacled super-villain had plenty to do, getting everything ready for the moment when he would launch the second Clementine missile and start an unstoppable global nuclear war. Every once in a while the tentacled super-villain would return to Spider-Man to gloat or to taunt him, then turn away again to continue arranging the devastating attack that would force the monarch of Latveria to strike out in all directions.

The chain around Spidey's waist was looser now. He took a deep breath, expanded his ribcage and pushed forward with his hips. Two links slid, one against the other.

"Now to see who's trapped whom," Spidey said.

He twisted his body so that his left wrist pointed at the viewscreen. The video pickup that allowed for two-way picture transmission was on the upper right-hand side of the screen. Spidey shot a glob of web-fluid at the camera, blinding the screen.

At the same moment he pushed again against the waist chain. It gave way. Spider-Man fell forward, his legs still chained. He shot a line of webbing at the ceiling, and pulled himself up. Up and out. His legs were free.

Spider-Man dropped to the floor of the silo. An access hatch led from the silo to somewhere back under the base complex. A sound came from the far side of the hatch. Someone was about to open it. The door creaked open on metal hinges.

"I don't see anyone," came a voice from farther back.

"Go in. The boss said to shoot Spider-Man. I'm going to enjoy doing that. He's helpless. I chained him up myself."

"Why'd the screen go blank?"

"Some kind of mechanical problem. There's no way Spider-Man could get free. Come on, let's go."

Spider-Man, perched on the wall above the opening, heard the entire conversation. The speakers came into sight: two more of Doc Ock's men, dressed in their typical black jumpsuits and masks, carrying automatic rifles. Spider-Man dropped onto them from above, flattening both to the floor. Their weapons fell from their hands, the metal clattering against the concrete.

With two swift blows, Spider-Man laid the two men out on their backs. Then the wall-crawler swung into the passage through which they had entered the silo.

"I'm coming for you, Ock," Spidey said. "There isn't a hole you can hide in now. I'm coming for you."

The tunnel branched. Spidey slowed. His spider-sense was tingling. The left branch felt like the more dangerous of the two. He headed that way.

The tunnel opened into a larger room, crowded with black-garbed criminals, all waiting for Doc Ock's orders. Spider-Man waded into them, fists smashing out. He leaped from floor to wall, swung on his web-lines to other positions, and entangled the crooks with ropes of web-fluid. His goal was the control room. He recalled how one minute had spelled the difference between defeat and victory earlier that night. He wasn't about to repeat that mistake. He struck again and again. Doc Ock's men struck him, too, but Spider-Man ignored the damage. He was strong, and he was fighting as he had never fought before.

Up on the satellite, Captain America looked at the sealed access hatch. Striking it with his shield would produce an equal and opposite reaction and launch him up into space to drift helplessly forever.

Instead . . . he looked at the laser mounts. They might be hardened against the electromagnetic pulse of a nuclear explosion, but they weren't hardened against a determined man. They were delicately mounted, in fact, to save weight during the satellite's launch.

Cap slid his hand along the smooth surface of the satellite. He gripped one of the lasers beneath its tip, twisted and pulled. The laser pod broke off in his hand, connected to the satellite by only a few strands of wire. It was still functioning. High-intensity laser light streamed from the top of the nozzle-like mount. Moving with infinite care, Cap pointed the ray downward until it brushed the surface of the satellite along one edge of the access plate. Metal boiled up in a cloud of silver vapor that quickly dissipated in the vacuum of space, and a furrow appeared in the surface of the plate.

Cap switched his aim-point to another part

of the access plate. Again metal boiled away under the attack of the high-intensity beam of coherent light. Now Cap held tightly to the satellite with one hand, and with the other he yanked firmly at the laser mount. The wire connecting it to the satellite gave way, and Cap let the no longer functioning laser drift away.

The gap where he'd melted away the metal was wide enough for him to insert the edge of his shield under the access plate. Keeping his grasp on the satellite, Cap pulled down on the other edge of his shield and twisted. The access plate broke off with a snap that Captain America could feel even though he couldn't hear it, and floated off into the darkness of space.

Cap looked into the hole he had made. There were the dials which would allow him to reset the codes. And at that moment, with a gentle sigh, his air gave out. Instead of the hiss of renewed oxygen from the suit's tanks, silence—total and absolute silence—was the only thing that filled his ears inside the pressure suit's helmet.

Cap held his breath and kept working.

Seconds later, he had successfully scrambled the codes. But the next part was even trickier. Cap carefully placed one arm through the straps of his shield. He had intended to use the tether to pull himself back to the quinjet while blocking the satellite's lasers with his shield. Now he would have to aim himself, feet first, at the craft, and hope they stuck to the metal skin on his first try. He wouldn't have a second chance.

Still holding his breath, he sighted the quinjet and pushed away from the satellite.

Spider-Man was through the last of Doc Ock's minions. The control room door lay just ahead.

He forced open the door. Doc Ock stood on the far side of the control room. The two firing keys were already inserted in their locks, thirty feet apart. Ock held one key in each of two of his tentacles. A third tentacle was poised above the firing button. The fourth tentacle lashed out, taking Spidey in the chest and shoving him hard against the concrete wall of the far side of the bunker.

"You've come so far, just to fail at the end," Doc Ock said. "Every time I have you in my power, you surprise me by getting away. This time there are no more surprises. This time I have won. Watch."

Ock turned the two keys simultaneously.

"Two keys at two different places. The designers of this system thought that they'd be able to stop any one man from firing a nuclear warhead that way. They didn't reckon on a man who has the arms to do it.

"Now you can watch my final triumph. After the missile is away, I can turn my full attention to smashing you into a pulp. No matter what the outcome, whether you die, whether you escape, whether even by some twist of fate you win our mutual combat, you will have lost the war, and the world. Watch!"

Doc Ock's one free tentacle pushed down on the firing button. Nothing happened. He pushed it again. Still nothing.

"What's the matter?" Spidey asked. "Something gone wrong in the world-conquering business?"

With that he fired web-lines from his wrists, aimed directly at Doc Ock's eyeglasses. Ock instinctively ducked, and the metal arm that had been holding Spider-Man slipped.

Spidey was free. He jumped, Doc Ock slapped him aside with a tentacle, and the fight was on.

CHAPTER
—11—

"**C**aptain America has changed the codes," Spider-Man said. "It's over for you, Ock."

"I will conquer. I must!" Doc Ock said, his metal arm whipping out toward Spidey's head. "Do you really think I only had one plan, one possibility? If you thwart one, another springs instantly to hand. I'll win all the marbles in the end."

"Speaking of marbles," Spidey said, ducking first, then leaping to the wall, "you're missing a few. Not that you've ever been too tightly wrapped."

Once again, Doc Ock's tentacles smashed toward Spidey. At the last moment the web-slinger launched himself into a forward somersault, ducking below Doc Ock's deadly tentacles.

"Little cramped in here, isn't it?" Spidey said, as a tentacle hit the control panel, smashing it open. Wires inside sparked, sending an acrid white smoke into the room.

Spider-Man threw a web-line to the ceiling and swung up as Doc Ock pulled his tentacle free from the wreckage and turned again to attack.

Spider-Man swung down behind Doc Ock, and roped one of his tentacles with webbing.

"Did you know," Spidey said, "that spider webbing is stronger, ounce for ounce, than steel?"

"Did you know that adamantium is the hardest substance known to man?" Ock replied, striking again at Spider-Man.

"Yes," Spidey said. As the tentacle swept by him he tied it to the first. Then he leaped up to the ceiling, then down again to the floor, webbing the two tentacles together. He spun webs around and around them, binding them into one package. "But I'm not trying to break them, just tie them up for a while."

The two arms, bound together, weren't able to strike from as many directions as they could individually, but they made a devastating weapon working together. Metal crunched and concrete crumbled wherever they struck, as Doc Ock aimed them again and again at Spider-Man. Each miss was a near miss, and each one seemed closer than the last.

Spider-Man, for his part, meant it to be that way. If only I can get Ock to think that he'll swat me with the club, he thought, he might forget for a moment to attack with the other two. And if I can get them, I'll pay him back for that special present he gave me out in Long Island. Ock isn't the only one who knows about electricity.

Spidey shot a web-line to one of Ock's free tentacles and pulled, running it across a piece of metal where wiring from the ruined control panel was arcing and sparking. He left the end of the line free on the floor. Then he tackled the other arm the same way, only leading it through a different panel on the opposite wall.

Then Spidey ducked, rolled, and came up in front of Doctor Octopus.

"You want me, Ock? Here I am."

Ock raised his bound tentacles in order to smash them down on Spidey. Spider-Man quickly shot a web-line to the uplifted tentacles, and attached the other end of the line to the two webs lying on the floor.

"Don't do it, Ock," Spidey said. "You'll regret it for the rest of your life."

"Regret smashing a bug? Not at all," Doc Ock replied, and brought his bound arms together, forward, and down.

The web-lines tightened, using Ock's own strength to pull his two free tentacles apart and into the smoking innards of the two wrecked control panels. Spidey stepped back as the clubbed tentacles smashed into the spot where he had been standing. At that same instant the electricity in the panels coursed through the free tentacles and into Doc Ock's body.

Ock convulsed once and then slumped to the floor, knocked unconscious by the jolt of raw energy.

"You said you wanted power," Spider-Man said. "Well, I gave you more of it than you could handle."

With a roar of engines, the quinjet descended to a landing. It flashed above the lighted base in New Mexico and braked to a halt on the landing strip to its west.

Captain America descended from the quinjet's cockpit to stand beneath the stars. The desert was cool in the pre-dawn hours. Cap took a long, deep breath and let it out slowly. He waited for a moment, then walked to the gate.

He was met by Spider-Man. "What took you so long?" the web-slinger asked.

"Taking care of a few details," Cap replied. "I figured you'd have everything under control down here."

"So to speak," Spidey replied. He jerked his thumb back over his shoulder to indicate a huge ball of webbing. From out of the ball protruded the heads of a good number of men, their expressions betraying various degrees of wonder, fear, and remorse. Doctor Otto Octavius's head protruded from the top of the ball, his expression showing only hatred and loathing for Spider-Man.

"You missed all the fun," Spidey said.

"Not all of it," Cap replied with a grin. "The Avengers aren't the only American force protected against an EMP. I had a lovely conversation with Nick Fury on my way back to Earth. You'll be pleased to hear that S.H.I.E.L.D. has defeated Ock's minions, wherever they emerged from their underwater bases."

"Hey—great minds think alike!" Spidey said. "I made a phone call, too, as soon as I discovered Ock's long-range signaling appara-

At that same instant the electricity in the panels coursed through the free tentacles and into Doc Ock's body.

tus. It was designed to withstand his EMP shot, so I was able to use it myself. In fact, any minute now . . ."

From over the northern horizon a moving wedge of lights appeared. It was a squadron of planes. They landed at the airstrip. Moments later, Spider-Man and Captain America were joined by a detachment of guards from the Vault, the ultra-high-tech federal prison designed to hold super-villains.

"I figured that if any other place in the country was shielded from an EMP," Spidey told Cap, "it would be the Vault. So I called the guys up there and asked if they wanted to make a pickup."

"Do you want a ride back to New York?" Cap asked.

"Sure," said Spidey. "In the aftermath of the EMP, they're going to need everyone's help." And, he added to himself, I know a stunning redhead who's probably worried sick about me.

Cap reached out a hand, and Spidey shook it. Together, they climbed aboard the quinjet. Moments later, they were airborne, heading east.

"Say, Cap," Spidey said hesitantly, gesturing toward the quinjet's communications equipment, "you think I could use the phone?"

Cap looked sternly at Spidey, then smiled broadly.

"As long as it's a local call," he said.